A Novel by Jerry Slauter

WOODCUTTER'S REVIVAL

5/7/13

Jasper,
God bless,

Illustrations by Scott Wiley

Printed in the United States of America

ISBN: 978-0-6156830-2-7
Library of Congress Control Number: 2012945895

Illustrations: Scott "Doc" Wiley | www.wileystudio.com
Layout: Wendy K. Walters | www.palmtreeproductions.com

Prepared for Publication By

PALM TREE
PUBLICATIONS
Palm Tree Publications is a Division of Palm Tree Productions
WWW.PALMTREEPRODUCTIONS.COM
PO BOX 122 | KELLER, TX | 76244

Contact the Author:

www.WoodcuttersRevival.com
email: jerrysworldsaving@me.com

DEDICATION

For Hannah, Hailey and Meliah

CONTENTS

ACKNOWLEDGEMENTS

My many acknowledgements go out to the following people who have been instrumental in the completion of Woodcutter's Revival:

My wife, Barb, has been the most influential contributor. She encouraged me through all of the valley's and mountain peaks of my life – all which were loosely based within the book. Not only did she live through these situations and encourage me, she 'put up with me' all these years. Barb has also been the one who knew of the project from the beginning and has continued to motivate me to finish it.

Gayle Schloesser has been a pastor and spiritual leader. Several of her teachings and research provided material to inpire some of the scenarios described in the later portions of the book. Gayle has also been one of the primary proof readers.

Of course, Scott spent over 360 hours illustrating the Woodcutter's Revival. The quality and connection to the story are obvious. Scott also contributed in forty years of friendship where we learned that people do grow and learn through conversations and long walks in Muncie, Marion, Anderson, Lafayette and Fort Wayne, Indiana. There were also some hikes into the Shenandoah Mountains along the Appalachian Trail in Virginia.

Dixie Wiley has posted the illustrations on their web site. She has also put up with both illustrator and author throughout the entire production and publishing process.

Tim and Shannon also did a major task in proofreading the early manuscripts. Shannon has also been willing to coach me in social media marketing. Micah and Melinda are always available to assist with my many technological issues. Why is it that adults are hindered by the computer and the information technology, while the youth can adapt in a natural seamless connection?

Alisha Burnette read the book and asked if she could share it with her mom. He mom then wanted to share it with Alisha's God mother. Alisha has provided encouragement, insight and assistance for setting-up my web site.

Wendy Walters has also been an encouragement and offered fantastic technical advice as the publisher. It has been inspiring to have somebody dedicated to the success of the writer, who is also knowledgeable in publishing books.

Chapter One

THE JOURNEY BEGINS

These were times when it was common for young men to leave the farm to seek a better life. Farms had come on hard times. Stewart Taylor and Raymond Warren knew the farms would no longer support the large families who had once worked them. Farms, in general, were either advancing into the Steam Age and needed fewer people or were being foreclosed upon.

They had been on the trail now about a week since Labor Day. They wanted to get an earlier start, around mid August, but felt they were needed to stay and help harvest the crops. The two, united by proximity and boyhood memories had sweated the furrows, put up hay, fed the chickens, and milked the cows. Both had survived the drudgery and the weather that was always too hot, too cold, too wet or too dry.

They had spent their entire lives in the valley. It was a unique western agricultural valley that averaged seven thousand, five hundred feet in elevation. They could see the mountains running north and south as they looked east or west from any point in the valley. Looking east from their home, they could see seven peaks of the Sangre de Cristo Mountains that were over fourteen-thousand feet and were snowcapped the year around. Looking west they could see the San Juan Mountains. Although they could see the mountains every day, they never had time to venture into them.

From the valley, Stewart loved to watch the sun rise over the Sangre de Cristo range. Some mornings the effects of the sun left the valley shaded and dark with the foothills resembling gray clouds. The illuminated mountains gained a red glow with each peak being very distinguishable. The clouds reflecting the morning sun from above and north showed a magenta sky with an azure background and gray borders. It was an image that he would carry in his memory, wherever he went.

They had different motives for leaving home and making this journey. Raymond was seeking his fortune. He knew he would strike it big. Although he did not like change, he was willing to suffer the inconvenience of uprooting and the unpredictable nature of the move in order to obtain his wealth. Raymond convinced himself that things would work out as he had hoped.

Stewart was a rugged optimist who looked for the adventure. He already missed his family but viewed the journey as a chance to see new things, meet new people and experience life. Stewart knew things would work out fine. Even if his tentative plans did not go exactly as he envisioned, he would make the most of whatever situation in which he found himself.

They were walking at a quick tempo, quiet, except for the sound of boots plodding against the earth. It was a brisk pace for having walked most of the day. They did not mind the fatigue or the uncertainty of not knowing how much further they might have to walk to find a suitable place to make camp for the night.

The two had known each other and played and worked together since early childhood. Their parents' farms had adjoined each other and they had been companions then, as now. They might have found themselves as traveling companions more by chance then by choice.

They considered themselves to be more like brothers than friends. Brothers have been best friends, but were placed together more by fate and genetics than preference. They also shared the common problem of the farm's inability to support large families. Whether or not they were best friends – they really did not know very many other young people - so they were traveling together.

Stewart was the elder of the pair by three years. He was ruggedly handsome with a large, square jaw and chin. His nose protruded as far in front of his face as his chin. Under Stewart's wavy hair was a high forehead with a protruding brow. His individual features would have appeared ordinary or out of place. Together, however the features appeared to fit together and enhance one another.

Stewarts' frame was large, but not disproportionate. His lean, sinewy arms and calloused hands gave the appearance of having worked hard for many of his young years. In spite of his rugged appearance, he had a soft, charming, childlike smile and reflective demeanor. The lengthy, brisk walk did not seem to tire his long legs, dull his wit or dampen his enthusiasm.

Raymond was slightly shorter than Stewart and considerably lighter in build. Raymond had no striking features, but was attractive. Nothing looked out of place. Raymond was not as excited about the journey as Stewart. He knew he could trust Stewart.

He wanted to leave the farm someday, but would not have left it at this time except that Stewart might be the only person who would be going through the mountains. Raymond did not want to settle in the small rural community that was twenty miles from the farm. He convinced himself that he had to leave the familiar countryside to strike it rich, although he did not yet know how.

The two had made small talk most of the way until late afternoon, when they were conserving their breath just to keep going. Stewart noticed that the small talk seemed to be a facade so as not to reveal too much about themselves or their hopes and ambitions. Stewart thought how little he actually knew Raymond. Stewart was not aware of the fact that Raymond was a little intimidated by his gregarious nature, his intellectual capacity and his physical capabilities. Stewart just wrote it off to their age difference.

As the afternoon shadows grew longer, they walked in silence, observing the unfamiliar terrain, noticing how their familiar farmland was now turning into foothills. Rocks were becoming more pronounced with each mile. The mid-afternoon sun began to reveal the details in the silhouette of the mountains in the near distance, rather than the familiar view from afar. Stewart broke the silence by asking, "What're you seeking in Wellspring?"

"Oh, probably the same things everybody else seeks - the ability to earn more than by farming, the possibility of learning at a college, and more girls than we could find around the farm."

"Are you sure that's the true order of your priorities?"

Raymond laughed and could not hold back a revealing grin that indicated he might have listed his priorities in reverse order.

Stewart continued, "I know that's what everybody says, but is that what you really want?"

"I guess so. What about you?"

"Oh, I probably want those same things, but I know there has to be more. It seems you can work for your whole life and earn enough to support yourself and your family, but what of it? Those who get more never seem to have enough."

Raymond, after reflecting upon the conversation, thoughtfully added, "I guess I would like to find peace."

"What do you mean by that?"

Raymond found himself a little defensive and offended that Stewart would not accept his answer at face value. "I mean I would like to feel secure and know that if, for some reason, I could not work, I could still have enough so I could eat, be comfortable and have nice things. I guess I would also like to be free from conflict."

Stewart responded. "When I think of peace, I think of something more difficult to explain. To me it means I would be doing the right thing with my life – like I am where I should be – not always wondering if I should be doing something else. That type of assurance would bring peace even in the midst of conflict."

Raymond asked, "How could we ever know?"

"I wish we could."

The attention of the travelers was diverted to the approaching dusk. Stewart mentioned they should start to consider where to camp for the night. They decided to set camp while they still had enough light to gather firewood and build a fire. After a modest supper of beef jerky, roasted nuts and some apples, Raymond said,

"It's been a long day and we have a long day ahead of us. We had better get a good night's sleep."

Stewart reclined in his sleeping bag, looking up at the cloudless night and the endless number of stars emerging in the darkening sky. Even though Stewart pacified Raymond by agreeing to try to sleep, he could not maintain silence. His mind was racing, "I just think of the possibilities ahead of us. I hate to sound trite, but our future is as limitless as the sky above us. Have you ever seen so many stars?"

"We need to sleep."

Raymond's response did not indicate his fatigue as much as different perspective of the situation. He could not sleep because he could only imagine the dangers and uncertainties that could emerge as they traveled further from the familiar valley. The thought of dangers seemed more real at night – not fear of darkness or what might actually be lurking out there at that moment. Rather, he envisioned himself facing these situations in daylight as if he were actually farther into the mountains at this moment.

He thought, "What if there are cougars or bears in the mountains? What if the passes have been snowed over before we get there? There could be highwaymen. We could run out of food or get hopelessly lost."

Once the two finally fell asleep, it seemed like moments until they were awakened by their thoughts. Raymond was awakened by his fears and Stewart by his enthusiasm. Stewart did not need time to shake-off the sleep before he was up and ready to talk. "Gramps told me about the battle the two parts of our mind wage against each other. It seems the thoughts we have when we first awaken reveal our true attitude toward life. Our subconscious is still active before the conscious mind begins to attempt to control our thoughts. If we wake up fearful about something, it might take several hours to shake it. If we are excited about something, we might not be able to contain our enthusiasm."

Raymond simply nodded his head and moaned in acknowledgement, "Uh huh."

They broke camp and resumed their journey. They walked for about half an-hour as the morning sun began to warm them. They soon smelled a faint aroma from a camp fire. After walking a little further they could distinguish the smell of coffee brewing and bacon frying over an open flame. "Good morning," hailed a stranger who was huddled by the campfire.

"It appears the two of you have gotten an early start on the day. Would you like some coffee?"

"Sure," Replied Stewart. "Our fire died in the night and we took no time to rebuild it this morning."

As they were enjoying the coffee, Raymond asked the stranger his name.

"Daryl Dailey," he replied.

Raymond said, "This is Stewart Taylor. I'm Raymond Warren.

Stewart asked Daryl, "Which direction are you headed?"

"Into the mountains, same as you," was the reply.

"Have you been through them before?" inquired Raymond.

"No, I haven't"

Stewart asked, "Have you heard of Wellspring?"

"Yes, I have."

"Wellspring!" added Stewart. "I hear tell if you gaze down on Wellspring at dusk, the light from the city reflects on the clouds like a candle on its reflector. She draws young men through those mountains like moths to a light."

"Yeah, I've heard something like that. Since I am traveling alone, why don't we team up?" asked Daryl.

"Sounds good to me," replied Raymond. "There is safety in numbers."

"The more the merrier," added Stewart.

Stewart and Raymond began helping Daryl. Stewart broke camp and Raymond helped pack his gear. The two travelers now became three.

Chapter Two

THE TRAIL DIVIDES

The three men traveled together for three days. With each step, Stewart and Raymond left their farmland further behind and the terrain was increasingly mountainous with no more traces of foothills. As they walked they kept the conversation light. Stewart and Raymond knew almost everything about each other – their families, home and backgrounds.

At first, they figured they would only be walking with Daryl a week or two and would then part company, so there was no need to get too familiar. Daryl and Raymond were closer in age than they were to Stewart. Each day, Stewart noticed the two seemed to be of like mind in most things they discussed. It was almost as if separated brothers had rediscovered each other.

Late afternoon, about the time they usually started looking for a place to camp, they came to a fork in the trail. They had been following a trail adjacent to a river cutting a valley through the foothills and a pass into the mountains. The fork in the trail appeared as another trail veered off along a stream that fed into the river. Raymond said, "It looks good to the right. It looks like we could stay on lower ground. You can't tell what might be ahead."

"Taking either trail would have its advantages and disadvantages." added Daryl. "Why don't we set up camp here tonight, decide on our course of action and begin fresh in the morning?"

After a tasty supper of beef jerky, nuts and raisins, they reclined near the fire to ward off the brisk night air. Daryl opened the conversation, "Raymond, you seem to want to take the safer route."

"Yes, it seems the traveling would be easier, and the weather would be milder. I'm amazed how much cooler the temperature gets the higher we go. Even though it's mid September, it feels like November would feel down below. You also never know what we might run into in the mountains."

"That's true," interrupted Stewart, "but think of the brook trout and the wild game. Until you are up there, seeing from the height, you really never know what view of the world you might have."

"That all sounds good," added Daryl, "but Raymond, who seems pretty logical, has good points for taking the lower route."

"Let me propose this," responded Stewart, "I feel safe enough to take the higher route, and you two would be safe, taking the lower route. We can meet each other in Wellspring in a few weeks."

Raymond argued, "You've never been to Wellspring. It might take up to Thanksgiving until we can locate each other."

Stewart responded, "Now we think we'll be able to get back up into the mountains any time we want. Let me tell you. Once we start working down in Wellspring, we'll never find time to get back up here. If we have the time it will mean we are not working and won't be able to afford to leave. I heard Wellspring is outgrowing nature and will probably even swallow up these mountains someday. Then there won't be anything left worth seeing."

Stewart knew he was exaggerating a little. He felt his argument had gained momentum and had begun to carry him.

Daryl added, "Stewart, you seem pretty independent, almost to a fault. I am sure you will be all right up here. Raymond and I will plug along and find him a place in town, um, in the city."

Stewart reluctantly agreed, although he had an uneasiness that no rationalization would overcome. Daryl smiled a smile that would have indicated a sense of accomplishment, had his smile not been shielded by the night.

They soon drifted off to sleep. Lying on the hard ground, the fatigue of walking good distances each day, coupled with the briskness of the mountain air made a night's sleep seem short.

Stewart was up before the other two. He was anxious to get back on the trail. Raymond awoke to the smell of bacon frying and coffee brewing. They ate breakfast and did not talk much. Each person thought any further effort to convince the other two of the soundness of their plan might actually have the opposite effect. It might have sounded as if they were over-pleading their case. They quietly finished packing their gear.

As they broke camp and bid adieu, they made their promises to meet in Wellspring in two or three weeks. Since the two plainsmen had no concept of the size and magnitude of the sprawling Wellspring, Daryl made a suggestion, "Whoever gets into town first, find an inn close to the trail head and wait. The other will be along shortly."

Stewart began his lonely trek. He soon lost visual contact with Raymond and Daryl. Although he was alone, he did not feel lonely. He felt strangely secure; even though he did not know if or when he would ever see another human being.

As he was walking, he was reflecting upon the parting scene with the other two travelers. Even though Stewart had been the one to suggest the arrangement, there was something haunting him about the way Raymond decided to travel with Daryl. He wondered why Daryl was so quick to agree to the separate arrangements. Could

Daryl have had some hidden motive in predetermining the separate routes?

Stewart attempted to convince himself that his impression was wrong. He could not think of a motive for Daryl to divide the two or to coax Raymond into taking the lower route with him. Besides, he did not think badly of Daryl. Even if he decided to turn back and attempt to catch the other two, he knew that would be almost impossible. He reassured himself that the fatigue, coupled with the altitude and the solitude were just playing games with his mind.

Stewart walked about three days and ate plenty of fresh brook trout. He was grateful for the extra food. To pack light enough for the length of the trip, there was not room for extra provisions. Sometimes, without the victuals provided by nature, he knew the amount he was able to carry would not be enough. He decided then and there that if God was able to feed five thousand with seven fish and some loaves of bread, who was he to question the Almighty's motives or ability?

Toward noon, about the time Stewart usually stopped for lunch, he saw a tree which had fallen across the trail. He thought, "That seems strange. Why would a tree just fall across the trail, and who would be around to cut it?"

Then he heard the moaning of someone in pain. As he moved close enough to survey the situation, Stewart found the source of the distress. The tree was pinning a man to the ground by his

left leg. Before he had time to ponder the situation, Stewart had thrown himself into action. He was chopping the tree in half a few feet from the man's leg.

The man was unconscious, but still had his color, so Stewart felt reasonably assured there was time to save him. There was no time to waste, as he needed to be treated for shock and the chills as quickly as possible. Within fifteen minutes the tree was chopped in two and the injured man lay on the path – barely alive.

Stewart gently placed his parka over the man and propped his head on the bedroll he had pulled from the pack frame. The leg was obviously broken, as it was bent in a direction that no joint would accommodate. Stewart made a splint and patched the man as well as he could. As the man warmed under Stewart's coat, he began to regain consciousness.

"Do you live close-by?" inquired Stewart.

Struggling to fight the pain, the man shook his head to the affirmative and pointed his eyes up the path to the left. Stewart gently carried the man in his arms. Fortunately, the distance was not very far. As they reached the cabin, Stewart was able to push the door open with his foot. He felt relieved when he was able to place the man in his bed. Although he now was reluctant to do so, Stewart knew he must set the break. He could see no signs of internal bleeding in the leg, so he knew the break was a clean one.

Stewart did what he had to do. Now that he had an old bed sheet to rip into bandages, he replaced the splint and attempted to make the dressing look a little more attractive. At this point he realized how effortlessly he had carried the man, but how extremely exhausted he now felt - both physically and emotionally.

As the man drifted off to sleep again, Stewart began to look around the cabin. From the cold ashes in the fireplace and the stale bread on the table, it appeared the man had been out of the cabin at least half of a day. He rekindled the fire and began to make some bean soup from a few slices of the cured ham hanging from the rafters and a bowl of beans that had been left to soak. After the beans and ham were cooking, Stewart found the tin of corn meal and made corn bread in the cast iron skillet.

While the beans were simmering and the cornbread was cooling, the cabin acquired the combined aroma of beans, ham, cornbread, coffee and a wood fire. The heat from the fire began to radiate throughout the room and he laid his head on the table. When he opened his eyes, the cabin was almost totally dark, except for the diminishing flicker and shadows cast by the embers from the waning fire.

At first he had no recollection of where he was or how he got there. Stewart fumbled around in the twilight and found the lamp in the center of the table. He stirred the glowing embers, placed fresh wood in the irons and soon rekindled the blaze.

Shortly, the man awoke. Stewart asked him if he was up to some ham and bean soup and cornbread. The man winced and nodded in the affirmative, as he struggled to find a more comfortable position. As they were eating Stewart began asking some questions. "How long were you under the tree?"

"I started cutting about daylight. That was my only tree I cut today."

"I am amazed you survived. You could have been done in by a wild animal or the elements."

"I learned a long time ago not to question some things. I am thankful when things work out."

Stewart asked, "Does anybody live with you?"

"No, I manage by myself. I have for the past four years."

"You know it's broken?"

"I had my suspicions."

"Oh, how rude of me. My name is Stewart. I'm on my way to Wellspring."

"Coming up from the farm?"

"Yes, how'd you know?"

"I've seen a lot of them coming through. Most of 'em go the lower route. My name is Michael, by the way."

"I am happy to meet you."

"Son, you don't know how happy I am to meet you."

For obvious reasons Michael already trusted Stewart. The trust was not entirely due to the fact of the sacrifice and skill Stewart demonstrated in saving Michael's life. Michael also trusted his ability to judge character. From his vantage point and his own past experience, he seemed to have a way of knowing people and being able to determine their motives. He knew he could trust his perceptions of people when he was wise enough to not allow his emotions to get in the way.

After eating, Michael drifted off to sleep. In the loneliness of the cabin and the awareness of growing darkness outside, Stewart realized Michael would need care and attention for some time. He entertained thoughts of Raymond. How would Raymond know Stewart was detained? Would he worry needlessly? Stewart also came to the stark realization that Michael would have died if he had not taken the high trail.

Chapter Three

DISCOVERY

While Stewart was busy in the cabin, caring for Michael, Raymond and Daryl reached a settlement in the mountain pass. The settlement was a small mining town named Discovery. Discovery had one mining company. The town had an inn where a person could obtain a bath, a room and a meal.

The town also had a general store, a boarding house, a furniture factory, a saloon, a livery stable, a church and a school. The boarding house was used by single miners who came to town and stayed a while. There were also several houses for miners with families to rent. All the commerce in Discovery was owned by one man – Edward Thomas. Edward liked to be called "Ned" by those to whom he allowed the privilege.

Raymond and Daryl had no trouble in deciding where to put up for the night. The inn was small and plain, but after a month on the trail, it seemed inviting enough. It was used by travelers who came to town on business or an occasional wanderer passing through. There were also monthly rates for those choosing to stay until they could obtain more permanent housing. Two of the six rooms were available, so they decided to check in, take a bath and meet in the dining room for supper.

Daryl was already seated when Raymond appeared. "Have you been waiting long? I couldn't pull myself away from the tub."

"No, I have only had time to have a cup of coffee and to take a quick look at the menu."

"How is the selection?"

"Limited, but the food sure smells good."

Raymond began to peruse the menu as he continued enjoying the aromas, the faint clinking of knives and forks, and the clatter of plates being carried from a nearby table. Daryl said, with a laugh, "This place sure smells different than Stewart's camp cooking."

Raymond, added, "The coffee is better too."

Raymond realized that he had not thought about Stewart much while they were busy surviving on the trail. Now that he had some time to relax, he wondered how Stewart was doing and how far along the trail he had advanced. His attention soon turned to studying the other faces in the dining room. The study consisted of quick glances at the other four tables, two of which were occupied.

The dining room was L shaped, with the smaller area being separated by a French door. In the alcove that was nearly as big as the main room was a vacant table, a sideboard and a hutch. The furnishings, including china, silverware and linens in the semi-secluded alcove seemed much fancier than the place mats, flatware and stoneware in the main room.

While he was wondering about the alcove, out of the corner of his eye, he caught the movement of another couple as they entered the dining area through the front door. The man took the woman's coat in a gentle but distracted manner. Raymond noticed an age difference as the man appeared to be about twice the age of the woman. Even though the woman was young in appearance, she exuded an air of self confidence in her mannerisms and the quality and style of her clothing.

Raymond felt that even though she dressed and carried herself so eloquently, she did not appear to be conceited or attempting to vainly convince herself of self worth. Raymond thought he had been sly in his observations until he glanced back at Daryl, whose face appeared ready to burst from the smile he gave Raymond. Raymond felt his face turning a bright red with embarrassment as he realized his observations were not quite as sly as he had thought.

The couple did not wait for the waitress to direct them to their seats but seated themselves in the alcove. As the French door closed behind them, Raymond could hear the waitress say, "Good evening, Mr. Thomas. How are you, Miss Victoria?"

"Good evening Sarah. I am fine, thank you. How is your family?"

"They are fine, thank you."

As this exchange took place, another conversation began in a whisper. "It is not polite to stare."

Raymond could not believe that he got caught staring again. After being so obvious and suffering the embarrassment of being caught the first time, he was so easily distracted and staring again. Blushing, he said, "I didn't think I was so obvious."

As the young woman was talking to her father, she casually glanced in Raymond's direction, noticing that he was a stranger in town. As her eyes made contact with his, Raymond quickly diverted his stare. When the waitress sidled up to the table to take their order, Raymond, nonchalantly asked, "Who is the young lady who came in with the gentlemen?"

Sarah answered, "She is Miss Victoria. I'd be careful about getting too nosey. Her daddy, Mr. Thomas, owns this town and he don't like any strangers asking too many questions – especially about Miss Victoria."

While Raymond sipped coffee and waited for his meal, he was amazed at how much he felt intrigued by Victoria. He could never remember meeting any person who had such an impact at the first glance.

Soon their meals arrived. They were so hungry for a home cooked meal they would not have noticed if the cooking was bad. On the contrary, the pork chops, corn, fresh bread and apple pie were very good.

After concentrating on the food for a while, Raymond asked, "What are your plans?"

Daryl answered, "I'd like to stay in town a few days and get rested. A person could become accustomed to accommodations like this real easy."

"That's a fact, but we can run out of money if we aren't careful."

Daryl grinned and casually, almost jokingly suggested, "We could check out the job situation."

At first Raymond was amused, but began to think, "That is not a bad idea."

After supper Raymond climbed the steps to his room. The room was very simple with a wooden floor, a well worn area rug, a bed, dresser, a night stand with an oil lamp, and a small wood stove. Raymond noticed a Bible on top of the night stand. Although the accommodations were not elaborate, with the experience on the trail, they seemed like luxury.

As fatigued as he was, Raymond thought he would go right to sleep. As he lay in bed, tossing and turning, his mind kept entertaining the thought of staying in town, at least for a short time. He thought he could work long enough to earn train fare to Wellspring, have a little spending money and arrive about the time he expected Stewart to reach town.

After struggling to sleep for some time he got up and lit the lamp. He reached for the Bible and started to read, "For whoever wishes to save his life shall lose it, but whoever loses his life for My sake shall find it. For what shall a man be profited if he gains the whole world, and forfeits his soul?" (Mark 8:36)

He laid the Bible back on the dresser. At first Raymond contemplated these words. He began to wrestle with them. "For what cause would be worth dying? More importantly, for what reason should a person live?"

Raymond did not like to miss sleep. He also did not like to interrupt his schedule, even while traveling. It seemed the harder he tried to sleep, the wider awake he became. He wondered why he had so much trouble sleeping when he was so exhausted, especially when he found himself in a real bed for the first time in a little over a month.

Finally, after wrestling with the verses he had read and considered every possible meaning, he drifted off to sleep. He slept longer than any one night he had spent on the trail. He was in no hurry to get out of bed in the morning, because he and Daryl had not set any specific time to meet for breakfast.

When he was finally fully awake, he figured the sun had been up for about a full hour. He was still not in any great hurry to climb out from under the covers. His room had no fire in the stove and the early-autumn night air had left the room with a briskly cool feeling. He could not shake the thoughts of the previous night. However, feeling his hunger and smelling the bacon frying from the kitchen below his room, he decided he could wait no longer to get dressed and go down to enjoy a hot breakfast.

After entering the dining area, he noticed the private alcove had already been set for lunch, while the other tables in the main dining area still had the trimmings for breakfast business. He chose a table near the window so he could look out during breakfast and take a better look at the town. He wondered how long he would stay in town and how he would fill his time. When Sarah, whom Raymond recognized as his waitress from the night before, came to fill his cup, he asked, "What does a person do to bide his time here?"

She responded, "Most people work six days a week. They ain't got time or money to do nothin' else."

"What kind of work do they do?"

"Well, in a silver mining town, most people go into the mines or they do the smelting. Then, there are the rest of us who run the inn, the company store, saloon or the livery. Those are all owned by Mr. Thomas. Then you have the railroad."

Just as Raymond's breakfast arrived, Daryl came bolting through the front door. He pulled up a chair and sat down. Raymond could not help but notice the enthusiasm Daryl attempted to restrain while he sat grinning at Raymond. "Ok, I give up. What are you trying not to tell me?" inquired Raymond.

I was just looking over the town. They always have openings in the mines. The pay seems good."

"Hold on. I am just passing through!"

"I know! I know! I was just thinking this is beautiful country. I don't know if a man could get rich, but sure could earn a comfortable living." beamed Daryl.

Raymond hadn't noticed that Daryl had gone from talking about a few weeks from the night before to 'earning a living' today. "Well, I guess it wouldn't hurt to check it out."

They finished their breakfast and exited into the street. Daryl led the way. The mining office was almost directly across the street from the inn. As they were crossing the street, Raymond looked back to the right and to the left. At the end of the street, he noticed a Victorian house with a picket fence. The house was the largest in town and the only one with a fresh coat of paint. All the other buildings had gray, weathered boards with the original paint mostly worn off.

"Who lives there?" Raymond asked.

"That is the Thomas Home."

Raymond looked back across the street at the mining office. Over the door was a sign that read, "Thomas Mining Company."

Raymond and Daryl entered the door and saw a clerk sitting across the counter from them. Raymond could also see two open office doors behind the clerk's area. He gazed complacently at the open doors when he caught a glimpse of a familiar figure of a woman as she arose from her desk. As he looked, attempting not to stare, he thought the clerk and Daryl could probably hear his heart racing. He was, once again, shocked that he reacted so strongly and out of control to an individual he had only previously seen once in his entire lifetime.

He could only calm himself by diverting his attention. It was too late. He could not restrain himself from glancing back at the open door and noticing the young woman, also peering in his direction with what appeared to be a look of intrigue. The next moment Victoria was proceeding through the office door. Her look of intrigue was now replaced by a look of impatience over the clerk's complacency in greeting the two inquirers.

"How may I help you?" she asked.

"We came into the job to check out the office situation...I mean...I." stumbled Raymond, feeling himself blush a brighter red.

"We would like to know if the mines are hiring." intercepted Daryl.

"Yes, we do have some openings now. Do you have any mining experience?"

"No, but I have done a lot of farm work."

"Well, stick around. Mr. Thomas will talk to you. He should be available in a few minutes."

Raymond, grinning, responded, "I'll wait."

As Raymond took one of the two seats in the waiting area, he wondered how he could be waiting to interview for a job he did not want. He verbally affirmed to Daryl, "Well, I guess if I get this job, I could work a month, earn train fare, and still get to Wellspring about the time Stewart arrives."

Hearing himself repeat his thoughts from the night before, Raymond wondered if he was attempting to convince Daryl or himself. Daryl smiled in acknowledgment.

Chapter Four

THE MOUNTAIN TOP

As Stewart was quietly fixing breakfast, he could hear Michael restlessly stirring, attempting to find a comfortable position. "How is your leg this morning?"

I don't know if it hurts less or if I am just getting used to the pain. Any position hurts after a little while."

"Breakfast is about ready. You are awake earlier than the first few days."

"That's why I'm awake. How could I sleep with the smell of your biscuits, ham and coffee? I think I am getting more rested, too. I wish I could go hunting with you today."

"I wish you could go too. I'm sure there are some things you could show me about mountain living."

"For a flatlander you are doing all right. Besides, I am in no condition to complain. Where did you learn your doctor'n?"

"On the farm, we had to learn to take care of almost any emergency on our own. If we could get a doctor or a vet, by the time they would get there, we pretty much had to have the situation under control."

The two enjoyed each other's company. Stewart had, as yet, not even learned Michael's last name. There had not been much time to talk at first. Michael spent most of the day either sleeping or eating light meals, when he was awake. When Stewart was not cooking, cleaning or caring for Michael, he was spending his free time learning to hunt and trap. He had no choice. His life and another's depended upon his ability to learn survival. Oh, he had hunted rabbits and birds on the farm, but that was recreational compared to hunting larger game in the mountains. Down below, he never had to worry about becoming the hunted.

Michael told Stewart how to make biscuits right in the top of the flour sack. He added the egg and mixed the ingredients until the mixture had the right consistency. He placed the lump on the cutting board to roll it out into noodles or biscuits. Michael was enjoying Stewart's cooking. He was also enjoying seeing the growth in Stewart. Michael loved seeing people motivated toward growth and learning just for the sake of enlightenment.

Stewart was beginning to gain some momentum in the management of daily tasks. He felt he could even coast a little now. He had put some game away and now did not have to spend all his waking hours finding and preparing food or caring for Michael. He even found time and energy after the chores were finished each day, while Michael was sleeping, to begin reading some of Michael's book collection.

Although they had not had much time to talk, Stewart was amazed how quickly Michael could get to the heart of the matter in conversation. Stewart was musing, while the biscuits were baking, how he looked forward to the moments when he had all his chores done and he could steal a few moments to converse with Michael. Stewart had never known a person with so many thoughts – thoughts that made Stewart's ears warm from thinking.

As they were finding more time to talk, the conversations seemed to have a great impact upon Stewart. Their congeniality was a combination of several factors. Michael had been alone for some time. Stewart did not know exactly why Michael lived alone.

Michael had obviously experienced much in his life and had time to think. Stewart had not been around an older person who had the time to just talk. Back on the farm, he knew his dad and gramps had many deep thoughts, too. But they did not have a lot of time to talk on the farm. He could remember when there would have been time to talk, it was better spent sleeping.

Stewart, even though he worked as hard as the older men, seemed to have a little energy left for reading at the end of the day. He read whatever he could get his hands on – which was more limited than he liked. Michael had a surprising number of books. From the appearance of the collection, they had been well read and had probably gone through some jostling to get them to the cabin.

Another factor that seemed to add to their growing relationship was the total dependence Michael felt for Stewart. He did not feel a sense of the dependency so much as a humbling feeling of being placed in the position of allowing another person to do the necessities he had always done for himself. For Stewart the feeling was like a type of bonding a doctor might feel for a patient. Stewart had never been in a position in which another person totally depended upon him.

Stewart did not mind being needed. He thought how he would have chosen to not be here with a stranger, if he had a choice, serving his needs and not being able to leave. He would have chosen to be closer to Wellspring by now, ready to get settled, meet new people and find opportunities.

He became philosophic about the situation and wondered how many of life's circumstances which are chosen for us are better than the choices we might have made for ourselves. He would not have known Michael. He also felt that he had to grow more from the unexpected experience in a few short weeks than he had previously in his whole life.

When breakfast was ready, Stewart placed the plate and flat ware on a board and took them to Michael's bed. He liked to eat with Michael and see the old man enjoying the fruits of his labors. "If it rains or looks like rain today, I will be back early."

"That would be good. You could get lost or sick in a heavy storm. Besides you're getting the food supply back up to normal."

Stewart enjoyed the mountain air and gathering from the earth without having to plant or harvest. As he walked, he thought back on the hard work of farm life. He could also remember how he and his family had labored too hard to make things work. He was glad his younger brother Nathaniel could take over for him while he chose to try a different life. In spite of the endless toil and hardship, Stewart missed the family. He also had a habit of mostly remembering only good things about a situation. He still had to remind himself that he missed Gramps because he had died, rather than just being home with the others.

While he was musing, he noticed the mountains seemed to take on a different appearance today. The rain clouds had always been welcome on the farm, outside of planting and harvesting time. Up here, they seemed to hover as a black menacing veil that at any time could release their burden. In spite of the awesome beauty of the clouds and the ruggedness of the mountains, the elements today were depressing. Stewart's thoughts bounced from good times on the farm to the warm fire and pleasant company waiting for him back at Michael's cabin.

Mountain life was hard in a different way. The actual work was not as long and tedious as farm work. There was a variety of tasks, none of which took all day long like planting and harvesting, but still had to be done. There were no neighbors up here to rely upon and no store to run to for food or any other necessities.

Last week he had to butcher a deer. After hanging the meat to age for a couple of days, it either had to be smoked or made into jerky. He had to stick with the task until it was completed or the meat would be lost. He was glad there was not as much meat as there was in butchering a full grown steer. At least with the steer, there were several people working on the project. There were more options with the steer in what could be done with the meat, too.

All of a sudden the dark rolling clouds began to pour down rain. Stewart had to decide whether to find a temporary shelter or attempt to get back to the cabin. If he got soaked, he would need the fire to prevent the chills. He moved in under a pine tree with heavy foliage. Close to the trunk, the rain was not yet reaching the ground. Rather, it was deflecting off the upper branches.

If Stewart stood in the right place, he only had to dodge a couple of trickles running down near him. As soon as he had time to position himself, the rain turned to a mix of rain and sleet. The rocks were becoming covered with a thin layer of ice. Walking on the ground would be safe, except where he had to climb through a small rock ledge.

While waiting Stewart thought how life in the mountains was dependent upon sacrifice. The animals ate grass, roots berries or smaller animals. If man lived there, he had to live on mostly animals, especially during the winter. Except for a little stronger taste, a leaner composition, and fewer trimmings, the food was really not much different than the food on the farm. However, on the farm, the animals were raised for the purpose of supplying man. Up here only the unfortunate animals supplied the needs of man or other animals.

Whichever way one chose to live, life depended upon death. The animals did not seem to mind belonging to the food chain as long as they were the predator and not the prey. With that thought he noticed the sleet had stopped and the rain was diminishing. He hoped by the time he reached the pass, the rocks would be clear of ice. He decided not to be one of the eaten.

As he inched his way along the trail, the rain stopped altogether. The sun began to peek through the clouds. That's the way it was in the mountains. One minute the sun was shining. The next it was raining and icy. Then the sun came out again. Stewart could see the rocks standing out in the sunlight. By the time he reached them they were almost dry. As he held on to the upper rocks and looked down at the narrow footing and shear rock face below, he was extremely thankful the rain had stopped and the thin ice had melted. He climbed through with relative ease.

As he entered the cabin, he could see Michael was asleep. He stirred the fire and added more wood, and Michael awoke. "I am glad you're back. I honesty became worried when I heard the sleet hitting the cabin roof."

"I was all right. I found a tree with good ground cover. I only suffered a few drips."

"You are learning these mountains well."

Stewart agreed, "I am starting to feel pretty comfortable up here."

"You want to be careful about getting too comfortable. Just when you get overconfident, something happens to set you back. Like this weather, fortunes can change in an instant."

Stewart responded, "My fortunes changed when I met you on the trail."

"So did mine – not just the fact that you saved my life, but you are helping me get though the autumn. This is the only time I get lonely. The dark clouds remind me winter is not far behind."

Stewart added, "I didn't mind winter on the farm. There were still things that needed to be done. We kept busy, but it seemed we were forced to be inside and together more during the winter. We found more time to read by a cozy fire."

Michael responded, "Oh, I don't mind the winter up here, if I have plenty of food and firewood. It's just these days when leaves have already changed color and begin to fall. Everything looks like death."

"Gramps always said, "Winter is not as bad as the anticipation of it.'"

"You know," said Michael, pensively, "That's true of most of what life deals us."

"Yeah, once winter gets here, the snow makes things seem secure. You don't have to worry about being somewhere else or doing something else. You couldn't if you wanted to. Even the animals that hibernate have no choice in the matter."

Stewart continued, "The snow on the farm reminded me of an egg shell – secure but within a delicate balance – vulnerable. We had already been through the depressing days of fall, after the harvest. The snow would then come and seal everything in, but you knew under the snow cover, life was beginning to form and would soon be out for the next year."

"I like that," responded Michael.

"Fall comes sooner and more drastically up here, doesn't it? asked Stewart.

"Did you say you had been up here four years?"

"Yep, give or take a season or two."

"You seem to like to talk to people. What would have ever brought you up here to live alone?"

"Well son, it's a long story. I thought I would have forgotten about it. I guess I just tried to keep the situation out of my thoughts. It looks like we have time as the weather is only getting worse. I uh, once killed a man."

Stewart tried to conceal his surprised look.

"I didn't come up here to escape from the law. There was no way I could have ever been blamed for it. I was the only one who could have known. I guess I came up here as a kind of self-imposed exile.

"At first, I just did not want to be around any people at all – not after what this man did to me. Then my feelings turned to guilt of not being able to forgive him or myself for my reactions. I had always talked about love and forgiveness, and did the opposite. I was shocked that I could lose control. I felt like a hypocrite."

Stewart inquired, "You are not hiding from people now are you?"

"In the last few years, I have not been here to hide. I have just become accustomed to living here."

"Don't you miss people?"

"I didn't think so, but after having your company, I am beginning to wonder how it will be when you leave."

"Who was this man? What did he do to you?"

"Whoa, one thing at a time. He was my brother."

"How did you kill him?"

"I beat him to death with a pick. That's where the story begins. We were partners in a mining operation. We were not equal partners, though because he had been the first to come into the mountains. Gold had already been pretty well played-out. We decided to go after silver. It gained no value until the gold was gone. He staked the claim and worked it by himself for three years before he finally struck enough silver to support himself and others. I was working construction in St. Louis when he sent for me.

"When he struck silver he didn't have time to dig, process and transport it. He sent for me and told me I could be a partner at sixty percent for him and forty percent for me. I thought that arrangement would work well for me since he had sold his horses to buy his mule, pick, shovel and supplies"

"I had my wagon from our parents' estate. We didn't get much else. We lost the farm because of poor crops and debt. When I first started working with him, things worked pretty well. We were doing so well he had to start hiring extra help – mostly drifters coming through who needed to find temporary work while attempting to stake their own claim or make their way to Wellspring.

"One small thing I noticed early, however, began to bother me. When he wanted somebody to do something, he would not ask. He would simply say, 'Get some supplies.' Or 'Take the load to town today.' He never said, 'Please' or 'thank you.'

"Dad was never that way. He was always nice to people whether they worked for him or not. I guess he believed that just because he paid somebody for their time did not mean he owned them or gave him the right to be rude.

"I could overlook the fact that my brother did not act like Dad. Things went along pretty well until we started getting successful. We had to build our smelter and begin adding more workers. It was one of the first wood-fired smelters up here. I covered the labor and he paid for material expenses for building the smelter as I did most of the work myself. That was fair enough.

"The problem surfaced in the way he began to act. When the two of us were working alone, he would joke and seemed at ease. When other employees were around, he seemed overly concerned about his image. It was like he wanted to demonstrate that he was superior to them and to me. If he truly felt he was superior, why did he have to go to such lengths to impress them with his money and power?

"I began to notice myself laughing nervously when he told me to do something. I did not know how to direct his commands, which should have been requests. He began to take greater efforts to impress others. He spent so much money on things we did not need, but things that would make him look or feel good. He liked new horses, exotic guns, gold ornaments and trips. No matter how much we produced, he was never satisfied. He was also getting pretty heavy into gambling and drinking. I think he was under pressure financially, too. He was using **his** money to build **his** town in **his** own image.

"I was able to stand it because he was gone more than half of the time. I also had my trips to get the silver to the depot in Junction. He would go to Wellspring or back to Denver, gambling – betting on horses and playing the cards. He also liked to impress naive young men who thought if they came out to work for him they might experience the same fortunes.

"He finally sent for his wife, Patricia and their daughter Victoria. That was when he really went overboard. He built them a new house and included a lot of things that were not necessary for the survival of their workers and their families. He wanted them anyway. Patricia was not demanding and did not require fancy things.

"I think he felt he needed to impress her. He built the church and went overboard, not so much out of reverence, but to gain her approval. There was no need for such a fancy cathedral way up here. He might have been attempting to buy his way into heaven. I always knew he did not really know her or other people. Most of all, he did not know himself.

"He wanted too much too fast. The longer I think about the ordeal, the more I realize he wanted the town to be a monument to himself, the town in the mountain wilderness he built with his own two hands.

"History was being written and he wanted to be part of it. The more powerful he became the more self-respect he attempted to demonstrate. It occurred to me, if a person truly has self-respect, he does not have to use all his energy to convince himself.

Stewart agreed, "That is true. I had never thought about it that way."

"He was beginning to look at me with suspicion. I think he could perceive that I saw through his act. After he brought Patricia, he stayed around all the time. I decided to get some space between us, so I went and joined Teddy and the Roughriders. I'll tell you more about that later.

"Before I left, we had an agreement. Since I had some equity in the smelter and built my own house, I would not lose any of the partnership. He tried to please Patricia, but love must have been blind. She either could not see his major flaws or refused to face the facts. She also kept out of the business, so she did not see how he treated people or managed the money. While I was gone, he lost Patricia to the flu that went around that winter. He sent Victoria back east to live with Patricia's sister Whitney and go to finishing school.

"When I returned, it became unbearable to be around him. He had to decide while I was gone whether he wanted to continue being a prospector or find an investor and become a miner. We would have to upgrade my wood-fired smelter to coal. That would require capital and a connection to the railroad. Both had their advantages, but he had to decide whether to remain autonomous and pick at the earth or get an investor and harvest the rich ore. He found an investor in Wellspring.

"I think he did not like the fact that anybody else owned even a small portion of the town. He and his investor were more like-mined than he and I. He thought he could someday buy out his investor. He could also perceive that I was not as easily impressed by his power trip, and after the war, I was less dependent than before.

"We had a shipment that needed to go to Junction. The railroad was not connected to town, so I was still taking shipments by wagon. On the way, I had a breakdown. My wagon wheel broke under the weight of the silver. While I was trying to fix it some highwaymen came by and pistol-whipped me. They took all the silver they could carry on their horses and the mules from the wagon.

"I lay there for three days, unconscious. A couple of hikers came through and found me. They said a deer was standing over me licking the wounds. It appeared that maggots had begun eating the infection on my scalp. The deer then licked the maggots off.

Stewart said, "Wow! You have been saved on the trail twice. The first time men put you there and nature saved you. This time, nature put you there and a man found you."

"That's true. I hid the remaining silver in the woods and tried to cover the broken wagon. Since I was closer to Junction, I walked in. When I got there, I wired my brother to get some money to pay my doctor bills, find a wagon and some mules, and get some supplies to return. His response was, 'That is not my problem. You were responsible for the silver.'

"I don't know if he thought I cheated him and kept his share of the money or if he was simply looking for a way to legally eliminate me as a partner. I had to find work in Junction as a contractor to get enough money to eat and obtain lodging. My expenses and doctor bills took everything I made for about three months.

Stewart sat listening, totally absorbed in the story. As Michael took a moment to rest and organize his thoughts, Stewart asked, "You don't think he sent the highwaymen to sabotage you, do you?"

"I have thought that myself, but I still choose to believe he didn't."

"Did you get back to the town? What town was it?"

"The town was Discovery. I had written several times to reason with him, so he had my address. He even sent me a bill for his sixty percent of the silver shipment. I reasoned that if we suffered a loss, there were no profits and we were supposed to both take the loss. He sent one other letter, stating, 'Your services are no longer needed.'

"Finally, I was able to get enough supplies for my return trip and pay the doctor's bills. I was able to buy Clementine. I just wanted to get back and claim what was mine, so I gave up on replacing the wagon and getting a second mule. I wanted to talk to him when I returned. I was still willing to forgive him and work with him if he could explain his attitude.

"When I returned, he had repossessed my house and told people I had abandoned him with a shipment of silver. He was conveniently out of town and would return in a few days. The cheating, I could forgive. The lying to me and about me, I could forgive. The fact that he would not reason with me was more than I could bear. I felt my nostrils flare. My fists clinched. I could think of nothing else. I seemed obsessed with what I was about to do.

"I remember waiting. Revenge was the only thing that kept me alive. I lived to kill him. It was dark. I was in the office. I heard his footsteps and hid behind the door. I felt the handle of the pick and lifted it. He saw me. I swung and scored only a glancing below. Then, sweet vengeance, he was alive and able to beg. I now had the final say. I lifted the pick and sent it and him home for good.

"Why did you say earlier you were never concerned about being found out? Didn't anybody see you when you were in town? Couldn't somebody piece the clues together? Were there more people who had as much reason to kill him as you did?"

Michael smiled, "Slow down, boy. You ought to be a detective. I could not be detected because the willful, premeditated murder took place only in my mind. In the two days I waited for him, I felt so disgraced by the rumors, I could not explain the real story to anybody. I figured I could always come back and actually do what I had envisioned.

"Then it struck me. It is easier to commit the act and deal with it than to rationalize it. I remembered my readings: 'But I say unto you everyone who is angry with his brother shall be guilty before the court.'

"I bought some supplies with the money I had been saving. Clementine and I lit out. The only direction I had not traveled from Discovery was up into the mountains, so that is where I headed. After two days walk, I found this cabin. There was a note on the door which said, 'Gone to Wellspring. I hope to return in the spring. If you move in, please take care of it. If I get back, I will want it back. God bless all who enter with a pure heart.'

"I came in but I knew my heart was not pure. At first I was shocked I could have thought of such an act, even committed it in my mind. I then began to thank God for not allowing me to carry it out. It took some time, but I finally was able to forgive Edward. I hadn't even thought about the situation for several years. At least now, when I remember it – because you brought it up – I feel no animosity toward him.

"I have even come to realize that all things happen for a purpose – even the things which seem evil. God can use it to shape and mold the victim. Whenever I get too proud of my piety, God can remind me of the potential evil in my mind. I only hope I get the chance, while I am alive to tell Edward I forgive him.

Stewart asked, "Have you had a chance to relate this story to anybody else?"

"Nobody has stayed this long before. Besides, whenever any other people have come through we always stayed busy. I guess I am on a self-imposed hiatus."

"What about the missing silver? Did you ever go after it?"

Michael answered, "Let's say, it is accounted for."

Stewart was attempting to comprehend the magnitude of this entire interlude. He could not shake the thought that the situation had been arranged by hands greater than his own.

"Michael, I feel you have taught me so much. I don't know how I could ever repay you."

"Hold on a minute! I have not taught you anything. I don't believe any man truly teaches us. It seems more like others help us confirm or rethink our own values. Now those values are probably planted by our parents and other significant people along the way. But they have to grow in fertile soil. Besides, I am the one who is beholden to you."

Stewart wondered if Michael was really in a self-imposed exile or if he just liked life better up here. He asked, "After all you have been through, how do you remain so peaceful and happy?"

"It seems we do not grow as people unless we have gone through some adversity. About peace, I am not torn by the doubt of whether I should be some other place or doing something else. Happiness to most people is either the hope they hold for the future or pleasant memories of the past. True happiness can only come from living in the present."

Stewart reluctantly had to excuse himself to begin supper. He had plenty to think about while he was preparing the meal. Somehow, he knew these thoughts would be like a star on which he would guide the course of his future. He would never be able to reach out and touch the star, but most of the time, he would be able to look up and see if he was going in the right direction toward it.

Chapter Five

RAYMOND IN DISCOVERY

Back in Discovery, Raymond had been working in the mines for almost three weeks. Although he did not like the work, every time he entered the mine shaft he felt less assured that he would ever leave Discovery. Even though he had sincerely planned to travel on to Wellspring he could not dismiss the haunting feeling that these mountains would be his home.

The miners worked five days for approximately ten hours a day, while working only six hours on Saturday. They rarely thought of their lack of free time. There was not much to do in Discovery. If there was anything to do, there was no money to do it.

All their clothes and supplies were purchased at the general store owned by Mr. Thomas. The people did not use real money. They used what was called the "scrip" system. Mr. Thomas had minted tokens of silver that were of about eighty percent of the volume of silver compared to the actual government coins that were in circulation at the time. That way, there were fewer temptations to take the silver tokens to Wellspring to convert into actual purchasing power.

Thomas owned all the housing in town. People paid rent with the silver tokens. This arrangement did not seem bad because, in town the tokens had enough purchasing power to live comfortably – just comfortably enough to not have time or energy to think about moving on. There was no comforting for the sickness – the malady from breathing the damp air filled with dust.

Oh, mountain air was clean and dry, but the air inside the cool caverns created humidity. The humidity was also a byproduct of men breathing and sweating in an enclosed area. The air was also filled with dust – the particles that were kicked up from blasting, digging and moving granite and quartz laden with metallic mineral deposits. The dust was a cloud that choked breathing at the worst times and stuck to a sweaty body at the best times.

There was also the sickness of the soul that hung over the miner. When he was not in the mine, he still could not get the dread out of his mind – the dread of going back into the living grave and not knowing if the narrow tunnel would become an actual grave.

As Raymond worked, he wondered when he would be able to catch a glimpse of Victoria again. He had not been around women much in his young life, except for his mother and his sister. Neither of Stewart's sisters, Margaret nor Kathryn, was close enough in age for there to be mutual interest. This was the first time he felt this strange aching feeling. While feeling the pain, he wondered why the thought of her also brought so much exhilaration, as he always caught himself smiling when day dreaming about her.

Most of the miners were family men. During the early prospecting days, almost all the miners were single men, hoping to send money back to their families so they could make their way out west to join them. As the mines became more settled in the process of recovering and smelting silver, the town became a little more family oriented and stable.

Thomas had an economic restriction on the ability to leave as the railroad would not take the silver tokens at face value. Unless silver prices were down, the miners had to earn about twenty percent more to convert the tokens into actual silver value.

Beside the reduced value of the silver tokens, the overall economy of Discovery ensured the miners' need to stay and work. Housing was provided and deducted from wages. After purchasing food and fuel, and they were able to save back a few tokens, there would be a need to purchase more coal or wood for the winter, or a new pair of shoes, work jacket or overalls. Thomas even hired some of the older boys to cut wood to sell to miners, as they had no time or energy to cut their own wood.

There was rumor of one enterprise created to keep the men occupied and interested in "civic affairs" when the gambling and liquor would not dull the pain or provide sufficient distraction. This type of enterprise was neither sanctioned nor prohibited by Mr. Thomas or the local church. It temporarily provided for companionship and comfort for the minors. Although everybody worked and did what they could, the only person who could accumulate wealth was Edward Thomas.

There was still the need to hire drifters who would work long enough to save money for train fair. Most of the people passing through were in search of something greater than spending their lives on the side of a mountain and working for somebody else. They were headed for Wellspring, which was just beyond the mountain range and down the river valley which flowed from north to south. Those who could afford the fare caught the train down. The spur line had been connected from Junction to end at Discovery. Those who could not afford train fare endured the walk down.

Raymond was beginning to wrestle with a decision to board at the inn, or move to the boarding house. He could also opt to rent a small house from Mr. Thomas. He did not like the idea of sharing a room with strangers, which might be included in the reduced price at the boarding house. He could still eat two of his meals each day at the inn, included in the price of his board, if he opted for the inn's monthly rate.

Renting would also mean paying extra for his third meal each day, skipping a meal, or doing some cooking on weekends, as he packed his lunch every day he worked. He was not quite convinced he was ready for that. There was also Daryl to consider in the mix, but he was not sure how long he could count on Daryl staying in town. Why had he been so easily swayed from his earlier determination to stay in Discovery for only a short time?

He decided he would ask Daryl if he wanted to share a room and split the costs at the inn. He found himself wondering how he had gotten so close to Daryl in such a short time. It seemed they had so many similarities such as background, age, temperaments and interests. He would ask him at supper.

After his shift ended for the day, Raymond returned to his room and washed his face and hands as best he could. Even after washing in the basin there was a residue of a mixture of granite and quartz dust, and silver ore that clung around his nostrils and gave his face a blackened appearance. The towel he used, although white, had black streaks and smears.

He was hungry tonight, more so than usual. The physical labor was beginning to catch up with him. The energy of his youth enabled him to find a reserve to recover during the first few weekends, and he was in good condition from farm work and the walk up. Any stored energy he was able to find was depleted with five and one-half long days of work with insufficient intervals of rest. His joints ached, too. He wished it were Saturday night so a hot bath would help soothe the pain and he would have an additional day of rest to partially restore his energy level.

As he found a table in the dining room he glanced, with hopeful expectation over to the alcove. Daryl was already seated and said, "Don't worry. I saved the best seat in the house for you."

Raymond, again, subconsciously glanced over to the alcove. Most evenings Victoria and Mr. Thomas dined earlier than the end of the shift. Tonight, though, there she sat. He gave his best effort to appear as if he did not notice her. He would sneak sly glances in her direction that would not be noticed as glances if she were not looking. He found that as he sat there, the glances became more frequent and longer in duration.

Either way, he felt himself blushing and anyone in the room would be able to perceive the reason. At one point he was able to, very nonchalantly, glance out of the corner of his eye. It was difficult to determine through his peripheral vision, but from Mr. Thomas' posture, he was sure they were discussing him. He wished he could have been invisible so he could go near and eavesdrop on their conversation.

Recomposing himself, Raymond said, "Daryl, there is something I want you to consider. How would you like to share a room at the inn? It would be nicer than the boarding house, but cheaper than rooming alone. "

"Sure! But I thought you weren't going to stay."

"Well, since I am not sure, the inn might be the best temporary solution."

"Temporary, as in you leaving or maybe trying to share a place with someone else in the future?" Daryl grinned as he glanced over to the alcove.

Raymond could not believe Daryl had broached the subject or had been able to detect his secret desires – so secret that he had not even admitted them to himself. But now he was happy the subject had been broached. He could not deny how he really felt.

Supper finally arrived, so he diverted their attention, at least outwardly, to the food. As Mr. Thomas passed his table to exit the dining room, Victoria smiled a pleasant smile in his direction. He felt uneasy as the brief moment their eyes met, seemed like an eternity. As uneasy as he felt, he could not look away. After she had passed, he sat awkwardly, with a silly grin on his face, staring at the door, forgetting about his hunger or his food.

Finally, the trance broke and he began eating. He felt embarrassed as he looked around the dining room. The other patrons attempted not to appear to notice, and be observed watching him in amusement and amazement. Raymond finished his supper, thanked the waitress and bid good evening to all. There was no use in attempting to downplay the entire scenario. He knew any effort to minimize the situation would only amplify the obvious to the observers.

As he returned to his room he felt the solitude and the emptiness the sparse setting seemed to reveal to his soul. He had felt homesickness, but this was the first time he realized what it was to feel loneliness. He reclined on his bed for a while, thinking and finally drifting to sleep. Thoughts of Victoria were filling his every waking and sleeping moment. Seeing her had not brought any relief, only intensification of the condition.

As he began to dream, he saw her walking toward him in a white gown, carrying a bouquet and wearing a veil. He awoke in a cold sweat. The excitement of such unexpected happiness quickly turned into despair as he realized the cold, dark emptiness of the room. Although fatigued, now he could not go back to sleep. He tossed and turned. The harder he tried to sleep, the wider awake he became. "How could she ever be attracted to me?" he thought. "Her dad owns this town. I am a stranger here. She knows nothing about me except that I needed a job when I went to work in her dad's mine."

Once he finally drifted off to sleep again, morning came quickly. As Raymond arose, he felt as though he had not slept at all. Raymond lit the lamp by his bed. As he regained his conscious thoughts, he said to himself, "It's only Thursday. The week is only half over."

He also reasoned, "If I am going to leave after a month, like I planned, that would be a week from tomorrow. Oh well, I am more than half way through."

Raymond had been in the shaft for about two hours when he heard the alarm. All he knew about the alarm was it meant there had been trouble in one of the tunnels and get out as quickly as possible. The community was situated in such a way that everybody could hear the whistle – similar to a locomotive whistle with a longer blast and shriller.

The whistle was mounted on the steam engine which drove the conveyor system. The ominous sound shocked Raymond as he had never heard it before. Once he realized, by the duration of the blast, that is was the warning, the sound became extremely annoying.

As he found his way out of tunnel number two, he could see dust still settling around the entrance of tunnel number four, the most recent shaft to be dug. There was a crowd of miners gathering around the semi-sealed opening. Some of them, like him, were from the crew of tunnel two. Most of them came from the other shafts or the smelter. There seemed to be some commotion and disbelief as people began to define the situation and determine a course of action. Raymond stopped beside one of the onlookers, "What happened?"

"The shaft collapsed. There are still two in there."

Then the foreman, Mr. Peters began organizing the onlookers. He told them to form two lines. The people nearest the opening began to hand rocks and debris to the person next to them and so on, down the line. This method seemed to be the best method to clear the debris in the fastest manner possible. Raymond, noticing that a great amount of the debris consisted of small rubble, began looking for a shovel and a wheel barrow. He also enlisted the efforts of Daryl, next to him, to grab the second shovel.

As he dug and removed the small debris, he could see a pick and bigger tools were needed. He enlisted another participant from the debris brigade to dig, while he looked for some bigger tools. Everybody else seemed to know what to do and worked quickly and without speaking. There was no time to wonder if their efforts would be futile. Most offered silent prayer while they worked.

They had to hope the two miners were alive, had enough air and had been in a secure place when the slide occurred. They worked for at least an hour, which seemed like an eternity. The slide did not appear to extend inside as it appeared from outside. As they inched their way into the dust and rock-filled shaft, there was some room near the top of the shaft where debris had not lodged into the top shelf. The small space extended several feet of the length of the shaft and all the way across.

Finally, about fifteen feet into the shaft, they reached a space where the slide began to diminish. It seemed they had dug through the greatest concentration of the debris and were now beginning to dig away from the center of the collapse. One of the rescuers shined a light through a small opening at the top of the slide. He could barely see two faces covered with dust. The only way he could perceive the faces was the whites of the eyes and teeth reflected in the light. "Are you alright?"

"Yes. We were in deeper, but the slide blocked us off here. We felt our way back to the back of the pile."

"Thank God!" Raymond exclaimed.

Soon, the debris was cleared enough for the two miners to squeeze their way out. They were hugged by their fellow miners in great celebration. As the rescue party moved out of the tunnel mouth and into the clean air, most of the town's people, who had assembled outside the shaft, let out a collective shout of joy and relief.

Mr. Peters noticed Mr. Thomas standing at the back of the crowd watching the situation. When the celebrating was finished, Mr. Peters announced, "It's closed for the day. Go home and get some rest."

As the rest of the people slowly found their way down the side of the embankment and into town, Mr. Peters increased the speed of his stride in proportion to the increase in his indignation. His anger came near to a boiling point as he stormed into the mine office. The clerk behind the desk could only look with amazement as he detected the rage Mr. Peters was exhibiting. He did not even bother to ask Mr. Peters if he could help. He knew Mr. Peters would find his own way into Mr. Thomas's office as he had in the past.

Mr. Thomas was talking to the Reverend Pharris. They both looked slightly shocked at the expression on Mr. Peter's face. "I told you this would happen. The time and money we saved by shoring at ten feet rather than six is going to get somebody killed."

In the past, he had attempted to appeal to Mr. Thomas's logic, by saying the gains made in less shoring would cost in down time and injury. Today, with the near loss of two lives, he was beyond logic and sugar-coating the truth. Mr. Thomas, attempting to diffuse the situation and appear to remain in control, in the presence of Reverend Pharris, replied, 'We can discuss this later."

"Unless you get those problems corrected and these tunnels safe, there will be no next time for me."

Now, Mr. Thomas, no longer able to posture composure, exploded, "Don't let the door hit you in the ass on the way out."

Mr. Peters shouted back, as he stormed out of the office, "Fine, I will be out by the weekend."

Mr. Thomas turned red with rage. He was not used to having anybody tell him the way things would be. He did not like it! Reverend Pharris did not know what to do to break the tension. He finally said, "Edward, have you done all you could to ensure the safety of the miners?"

"Listen, Preacher, this is my town. The only thing I don't own is the church, but we both know who supports it. You take care of their social needs and I will take care of the rest."

"I understand. I know you contribute more than the rest combined. I will be on my way now. Oh yes, may um…, may God bless you."

The next morning Edward and Victoria were in the office very early. "Father, how could you let Mr. Peters walk out? He was a very valuable employee and a leader"

"Nobody is irreplaceable."

"No, but they all respected him."

"They respect me!"

"Father, they fear you. How far would they follow you because of fear? They would have followed him to their death. It is not respect when people do what you say because you have power over them."

Mr. Thomas growled under his breath in exasperation, "Ugh, do you ever remind me of your mother! Nobody crosses me and stays here. It is my way or the railway. Young lady, I would not let you stand there and talk to me this way if you weren't my daughter."

Victoria knew she was the only person who could reason with him. She also knew she was reaching the limit of where she could press the issue. Simply because she was able to express her view did not mean her words would be heeded or even considered. She was beginning to question that if he was so strong, why was he so afraid of allowing anybody to break through his veneer. She was also beginning to understand that actions postured as self-respect were actually attempts to gain or convince himself of respect by dominating others.

Victoria began to reintroduce reality into the situation, "Enough of worrying about what happened. We need to consider what we are going to do. Since people respected Mr. Peters, we will have to be careful what we say and what steps we take to replace him."

Mr. Thomas interjected, "If we try to use one of his friends, they will undoubtedly know the alleged problems he has discussed with them. We need to bring someone in who is intelligent but unaware of the way things operate, naive."

"You mean someone you can control?"

"I was thinking more in the lines of someone we could train into our way of thinking and mold him into a leader."

Victoria had never seen Edward perplexed like he was today. She had a sudden realization of fear that the man she most admired in her life might have strongly different ways of thinking about how people ought to be treated than she had. "But, who could we find, Father?"

They both thought of the same person, but were reluctant to offer their thoughts for fear of what the other might say. Their motives varied, also. Mr. Thomas thought a young, well-read man, with work experience, in what might be considered a family business, might be easier to control and shape into his own image than one of the local people.

He had not spent any extra money educating these people for more than just the expense. Oh, he provided a school, but that was more to indoctrinate than to educate. He feared that the more people were educated the less they tended to be controllable. He had justified this belief by referencing that Fredrick Douglass, a slave who broke the law by educating himself and becoming a writer and orator was able to get the anti-slavery message out.

Victoria's choice reflected the belief that the young man might have some potential – maybe personally and professionally. She justified her position by stating, "Did you notice how that, I think his name was Raymond, took charge and kept a cool head in the emergency?"

Edward said, "There is one other problem we have to discuss."

"What is that?"

"Apparently, and coincidentally, our school teacher, Kimberly Knox has given notice. I never would have guessed she would leave when Mr. Peters left," Edward said as he gave Victoria an overly dramatic wink of the eye.

"Well, she was only renewed with reservations last year. We were going to have to dismiss her this year anyway. She signed on last August, but did not report to work until two weeks before Thanksgiving. She was warned several times about being considered the town gossip by sharing confidential information about students and their families. She was like Mr. Gradgrind in Dickens's novel, *Hard Times*. She thought she could reduce education to a mathematical equation. She thought she could convey all facts without appealing the emotion of the learner. What was her reason?"

Mr. Thomas replied, "She says she is going to take an administrative position down at South West School of Education. She will be leading a faculty of seventeen teachers and professors. How would you like to work for her?"

"Not if she leads the way she taught. Besides, I think we are talking more about controlling and managing the faculty, not leading them. You have to know something about education and learning to lead other teachers," Victoria said.

At breakfast, Daryl came down in his traveling clothes. Raymond asked, "Are you going to work in those today?"

"No, I am on the ten fifty-five out of here. I cannot go back into that grave with only one open end."

"I wish I could convince you to stay."

"No, I have been thinking about this since we got here. I have to go. I wish you and…the others all the best."

Raymond finished breakfast quietly and shook Daryl's hand as he left for work. He said, "Thanks for going through the mountains with me. I will see you when I get to Wellspring."

Daryl offered a doubtful grin and said, "Good bye."

The miners finished the week on a status-quo basis. There were several rumors about what happened to Mr. Peters, but no official word. People who knew what happened were not talking, at least not publicly.

On Monday, as Raymond reported to work, there was a note that directed him to go to the office to talk to Mr. Thomas. He recognized the writing on the note and beamed. As he headed toward the office, his joy turned into apprehension. They had probably decided they did not need his services any more. That would be fine. This was the week in which he planned to leave any way. He had not saved enough for train fare. How much would they pay him for the time he has already worked? Would he have to walk to Wellspring? If he had to walk down, did he have enough to buy supplies? "I wish we were paid in real money or actual value in silver rather than these stupid tokens. With this much time passing and the walk down, how would I find Stewart?"

Upon entering the office, the clerk told him Mr. Thomas would be right with him. The door to Mr. Thomas's office was standing open and as soon as he saw Raymond, he said, "Come on in."

Victoria was in the office and Mr. Thomas closed the door. 'Raymond, we have been noticing your performance."

"I can explain. It was an emergency. I acted out of instinct. I can learn more."

As he defended himself, Raymond began to realize that he really wanted to continue working in the mines. At least, if he was leaving, he wanted it to be his choice, not somebody else's.

"Oh, you misunderstood," laughed Mr. Thomas. "Mr. Peters is no longer with the company. We thought we might train you to work in the position of foreman."

"Thank you for the compliment, but I am not really qualified."

"Oh, don't be modest. You have worked all your life in a family operation. That is what we want you to do for us. Help us run our family mines. Like I said, we will give you all the training and support you need."

"But, there is so much to learn. I don't know if they will accept me."

Victoria responded, with almost mechanical repetition of a phrase she had heard her father repeat, "With no risk, there is no courage. Without adversity there are no heroes."

Then she brightened, almost as if she had a sudden revelation, "Besides, I hear you acted heroically, during the aftermath of the cave-in."

These words from anybody else would have seemed cliché. Raymond knew he had only acted logically and found something that would speed the rescue. From Victoria the words shot straight into Raymond's heart, overriding any logic or defense he had considered. The words acted as a magic elixir, bolstering any real courage he lacked.

Victoria, below the conscious level, in the deepest recesses of her mind, might have been subconsciously seeking a new hero.

Chapter Six

THE ESSENCE

Michael appeared to be enjoying his time of recovery. Stewart's cooking was improving and he was able to keep ahead of the food supply and the daily tasks necessary for survival. There was collecting water from the stream, splitting and stacking wood, tending the fire, cooking and cleaning. Michael was beginning to get rested so he was awake more hours a day than Stewart. The time they both cherished most was when all the activities were completed and they had some occasion to talk. Michael never wasted time on small talk. Stewart almost felt as if Michael already knew everything about him without having to reveal many facts.

Michael seemed to have boiled down the elements of life to the essence. He had so much time to think, read, and pray without a lot of distractions. He had even tried his hand at writing. He was a patient man and had mellowed with age. As he grew older, he also came to the realization that time grew shorter each day and there was no retrieving any lost hours, days or years.

He was not afraid to cut to the quick in conversation. If a statement was made without much prior thought or one that might have required a further exploration of facts, he would ask direct questions. Stewart wondered if it would be this way back down in the flat lands or if he and Michael found themselves in "normal" circumstances.

Michaels' philosophical challenges could make you rethink your position without causing you to feel like a fool. Stewart remembered his gramps saying, "Small people talk about people. Average people talk about things. Great people express ideas."

By those standards, Michael was the embodiment of intellectual greatness. Stewart considered what an unfortunate situation it was for all this knowledge and wisdom to be locked in this cabin with no way of sharing it with mankind. Stewart hoped, later after some schooling and more life experiences, he would dedicate himself to expressing the growth and insight he had experienced while on this mountain. Maybe he would write.

"Michael, do you ever think about death?"

"I would rather think about life. We all will face death. There is no sense in reducing the quality of life worrying about the inevitable."

"Do you ever regret about the time you have been isolated and away from," Stewart fumbled for words, "life?"

"By life, do you mean the way most people live?"

"Yeah, I guess so. That, and being around others with whom to share your experience."

"I feel I have drawn closer to life. When you are around other people, you need to think their thoughts and believe their ideas as your own. You accept the way most people do things as 'normal.' Normalcy is dictated by trends in style, convenience, preference or necessity.

"No, I do not feel the years I have spent up here have been wasted. To find what life is really about we must decide what is important. It is very difficult to prioritize your values in the flowing and changing current of society. If you have a chance to get away from the attainment of wealth, getting ahead and being successful for long enough, you realize these goals were not that important. When you realize what is really important, you have a changed perspective."

"What is really important?" inquired Stewart.

"As you grow older, you find only things that really matter are those things you cannot accumulate, but conversely the things nobody can take from you. The only way I can explain is through a story. Have you ever ridden on a train?"

"Yes, we used to ride the train to visit relatives back east. We would get on one day, ride for about two days and arrive at the station a few hours from their house."

Michael smiled and continued, "Most people ride the train just like they live life and do about anything else. They just get on and later, they are where they think they are supposed to be. Those tracks did not just grow there in the wilderness. When the first track came through, I was about your age. There was a need for ties for the roadways to support the tracks. The railroad used to contract the work so they wouldn't have to buy the wood and cut it. Instead, local people with stands of timber on their property would cut the lumber, saw it to dimension and deliver it to the proper location along the track constructions sites.

"Farming was progressing well enough and we had a stand of trees on the place, so I was able to make some spending money by selling ties to the railroad. That was where I first learned the lesson – everything of value has a price, but not all things that are high priced have value.

"During construction, trestles had to be built over the river ways and connecting mountain passes. Tunnels had to be blasted through solid rock. The work was dangerous. Conditions were rugged and bleak. Several workers lost their lives. Most of them aged more than if they stayed in the comfort of their homes. Those who were on the road the longest were away from family and loved ones.

"Someone got the idea to import Chinese workers as they were skilled in the use of black powder. The railroad people had to convince the workers that the benefits of life in America outweighed the sacrifice and risk. That is for the workers who were brought here on their own volition and legally. Nobody knows how many workers were kidnapped and forced into labor. It probably helped that the language barrier obscured these facts.

"We do know that overall, there were an estimated one thousand-two hundred Chinese workers who lost their lives on the railroad construction. Some days, they blasted through the mountains and only gained eight inches of progress. Some days they tunneled through snow to continue working. I was told of an incident when the snow tunnel collapsed and buried the workers.

The tunnel was cleared and the bodies that were not in the way of the track were not recovered until the snow began to melt in the spring. The workers would work extra hours, when they had them, recovering the bodies because the Chinese man wanted to be buried in his home soil.

"Most of the American workers who started on some phase of the project only saw a segment completed. Very few of the workers were able to go the whole distance. The progress of those who came later was built upon the efforts of the earlier workers.

"Now people can travel smoothly and effortlessly, at about six times the speed of a fast horse. As the horse and rider wear down quickly, the train moves on, seemingly, almost effortlessly. In fact, you can even get rested while riding on the train. Very few of the people who ride on those narrow ribbons of steel realize the sacrifice made by the individuals building the track. Now they carry cargo, medicine, supplies, books, teachers, judges, preachers, and everyone in search of a dream. The rails reunite families and have as many good purposes as you can imagine.

"That is the way life is. We are each given only a short segment of the total continuum. Some have it better than others. Some put their time into better use. If we worry or fret about the section we didn't get, or grumble about the one we got, our short segments will be over and we will not have even realized it. That is the way my exile has been. Sure, I have missed a lot of things I would have experienced down there, but I would not trade the things I have gained. Besides, an experience is never wasted if you learn from it, and no lessons are free of cost.

"We gain from others. I guess I am riding the tracks you built," observed Stewart.

"That's the point I was making, not so much that you have ridden on my tracks as much as, we all benefit from the wisdom and the technological progress of others and have responsibility to pass on what we have learned."

Stewart was amazed as he thought back to his original intentions in initiating the conversation. He only wondered how he would ever be able to continue Michael's track or fuel his own locomotive so others could ride it the furthest.

After a few moments of thought, Michael added, "Our lost years are only restored as we cause others to benefit from them. Have you ever read the prophet Joel?"

Stewart responded, "I have, but I really couldn't tell you what I learned from it."

"There is a passage which says, 'Return to Me with all your heart, and with fasting, weeping and mourning, and rend your hearts and not your garments…then I will make up to you the years that the swarming locust has eaten, the creeping locust, the stripping locust, and the gnawing locust.'

"The swarming locusts are all those burdens which seem to overwhelm us. The creeping locusts are the thoughts we hold in our minds and never know how they got so entrenched there. They are the thoughts that keep us awake at night or the thoughts that cause our hearts to jump or our stomachs to sour when we awaken. They are fears and worries. The stripping locusts are the problems that arise after we think we cannot carry another burden. Finally, the gnawing locusts are the concerns which take our joy and cause us to be melancholy.

"Do you notice all these are feelings or perceptions? They are not the actual problems or dangers, themselves, only the way we perceive them. After we get ourselves straightened out, the problems and the risks remain, but we see them differently and feel as if we have help with them.

"Let me give you an illustration. Our spiritual life is like cutting wood. We can go into the forest and cut wood alone or with the help of others. We then drag or haul the wood to the wood lot and split a stack. The wood burns best when it has been seasoned. There is only one way to season the wood. That is time."

"Only after all the effort can we warm ourselves with our fire. We were warmed by the efforts of cutting, hauling, splitting and stacking, not to mention building physical strength and stamina. But we are comforted, with little effort, along with comforting others if we put our efforts into maintaining the fire.

"A good fire results from time and preparation. Fellowship is like fire. You have the most to contribute by the hours you have spent in preparation – like cutting the wood – the reading, praying, meditating, writing. You can then help others by removing the dead ashes and stirring the live embers occasionally.

"Michael, you have definitely stirred my fires. How can I help others?"

"That is something we all have to discover for ourselves. We were given talents and desire to use to the fullest. We will benefit most from them as we find a means to allow others to benefit."

Michael thought a little more and added, "I have read through the Good Book several times. One principal mentioned over and over again is justice, mercy and defending the rights of the defenseless. When I was down there, attending church regularly, I can never remember a preacher even mentioning these concepts. That is what restoration is all about and making up for the years the locust have stripped. It is revealing the wrong, reviving the wronged."

"Do you think living like you describe increases the number years of your life?"

"Yes, but I have discovered that it is not as important how we live as why we live."

Stewart looked dazed with all the information he had just encountered, he was not sure if he would remember it all. He knew if he forgot the words, the thoughts and motivation would remain with him. "Look, Michael, the sun is coming up."

Chapter Seven

RAYMOND AND LEADERSHIP

Raymond had been the foreman-in-training for a week. Mr. Thomas had cautioned him that the miners would be resentful, envious and possibly hostile toward a flatlander coming in and stepping right into a leadership role. He had warned, "They might feel as if they have put more time in and deserved to be considered for a leadership position."

Raymond was a little surprised how well the miners accepted him in his role. Possibly, Mr. Thomas put more weight into the leadership position than did the miners, or maybe, he was not as attuned to their thoughts as he imagined. Maybe Raymond was just a likable guy. Maybe the miners put a lot of weight into the fact that Raymond acted with a calm and cool head in the cave-in.

In reality, were these men potentially placing their health, safety and very lives into the hands of anybody who was a leader, either designated by the ownership or not? It could have been that the miners perceived that nobody, regardless of title was a boss in Mr. Thomas' organization except Mr. Thomas.

Mr. Thomas instructed Raymond to work along-side the other miners for a while. His first supervisory task was to verify the working time of the miners and watch to make sure they were meeting quotas. Raymond, in his naïveté, thought any progress into those rocky caverns was tremendous. The miners knew how much conditions could vary between solid rock that had formed into one huge mass and the veins which were loosely packed rubble between two mammoth shelves. The silver was more difficult to break out of the solid rock and more likely to be found in the looser rubble. They had to break and blast through the solid masses to get to the veins.

The miners knew what Raymond was assigned to do. He was surprised how much they began to discuss working conditions and compensation with him. He actually began to feel as if he could make a difference. He could be a voice to Mr. Thomas so their concerns could be heard by ownership.

The miners had seen others come and go while attempting to "grow" into leadership roles. They knew Raymond would be asked to repeat everything he heard them mention. The miners were aware that the quickest way to express their concerns to Mr. Thomas was to allow Raymond to overhear them. They realized Raymond would repeat their concerns, but were unaware of his sincere motives for doing so.

They also knew how to "snow" the inexperienced foreman by loading some extra rubble into the carts before they passed by his scrutiny. They were not dishonest. They believed in giving a full day's work for a full day's pay. They also knew how to survive with an unreasonable boss who might measure the wrong criteria for progress, assign capricious and arbitrary standards, and would not listen to reason.

They knew Mr. Thomas was more inclined to measure performance in terms of demonstrating honor toward him than actual rocks moved or silver extracted. He also tended to try to find underlings who would show him outward signs of honor and who would expect the same in return from the other miners.

Although Raymond only knew Mr. Peters for a short period of time, he was aware he had some huge shoes to fill. Raymond often, in filling the time of tedium and boredom with some mental stimulation, compared himself to Mr. Peters. He knew Mr. Peters was one-of-a-kind, because he truly cared for the well being of the men and their families. Although Mr. Peters never attempted to offer opposition in the form of confrontation or public debate, Mr. Thomas was careful to avoid any open verbal encounters with Mr. Peters.

The miners had trusted Mr. Peters, as they knew he was genuine. Possibly, if he had attempted to resist Mr. Thomas' bull-headed ways in front of the miners, they would have suspected that he was posturing his resistance to gain their respect and trust. He would also have not lasted long if he attempted to make a habit of confronting Mr. Thomas in public. The miners missed Mr. Peters. Although Mr. Thomas would never admit it, his organization was better off with Mr. Peters than without him. Mr. Peters did not have to demand work from the miners. He knew how to encourage them even with the paltry amount they earned in actual pay or benefits.

With the sudden departure of Mr. Peters, Mr. Thomas seized on the chance to use the incident to accomplish some major organizational changes. With the appointment of Raymond, he had some duplicity of purpose. He felt as if he had an ace up his sleeve with a new leader, as he could introduce the "new method," train the new foreman and make the miners more dependent upon the foreman to succeed. As the mines were becoming less and less productive and new methods of mining were becoming common practice, this would be the time to shake the miners' comfort zone and allow the new leader to make a major contribution in the new system.

Mr. Thomas asked Raymond to come over for dinner on Sunday. They would take some time after dinner to discuss Raymond's progress and help with a further course of action. There was no way he would use company time or sacrifice his own evenings to have a management meeting with Raymond.

Raymond thought they would be meeting in the dining room at the inn. He was pleasantly surprised when he learned they would be dining in the Thomas home. Surely, Victoria would be home on a Sunday afternoon, not that the thought of her concerned him in any way.

"Come in Raymond. Father, I mean Mr. Thomas is in the living room."

When Raymond arrived, Mr. Thomas was sitting in the living room, comfortably in his huge leather winged-back chair, reading and smoking his pipe. The fireplace was burning, giving the smell of mountain aspen.

Victoria was wearing a lace apron over her usual elegant attire. She looked slightly out of place in her domestic role. It might have been that Raymond usually saw women wearing more casual clothing to do work around the house. It could have been that Raymond had only seen her as a tough, clear-headed business woman – her father's prodigy. He could not say he minded the unexpected and pleasant change. The coziness and aromas of the pipe tobacco, the wood burning and the smell of baked ham and sweet potatoes almost lulled Raymond into a trance.

Although Raymond was beginning to feel a little familiar around the Thomases he could not yet say he felt comfortable. He could not decide if the discomfort was from Mr. Thomas' seemingly cold demeanor, or his feelings he knew he could not hide from Victoria. He was happy to admit to himself, that it was a combination of both perceptions.

"Hello, Raymond," said Mr. Thomas, without getting up or offering his hand to shake. "How has your first week gone?"

"Father, business talk can wait until after dinner."

"Dinner sure smells good, Miss Victoria." Raymond added to break the tension.

"Raymond, you can call me Victoria."

Raymond attempted to make some small talk, without much assistance from Mr. Thomas, while they waited for dinner. He could not think of much to say and wished he could be helping in the kitchen, not that he enjoyed kitchen work. Finally, after what seemed an eternity, which could have been due to the hunger, the aromas or the tension, Victoria announced, "Dinner is served."

Raymond could not remember how long it had been since he had an honest-to-goodness home cooked meal. Oh, the inn was good, but cooking in the volume which they had to serve each day did something to the food. Trying to keep the food warm for serving in shifts had also limited the appeal of the food. This meal was cooling on the table directly from the oven. Victoria had done justice to the fixings. After dinner she served an apple pie from the apples that had recently come by rail. "If this was my last meal, I would die a happy man!"

"Oh, thank you, Raymond, I enjoyed fixing it."

With the taste of the meal, the smell of coffee and hearing her pronounce, "Raymond," he found himself in another trance. The trance was interrupted abruptly by Mr. Thomas, "Now, Raymond, if Miss Victoria will permit, we can discuss business over coffee."

"The miners are accepting me better than I thought they would."

"That is good. For now, I want you to proceed as you are, accepting more responsibility as you progress. Pretty soon we will have you supervising and you won't have to do the actual work."

"You will still want me to do mining work won't you?"

"Not really. You will need to gradually isolate yourself from them. They will take you for granted if you remain one of the boys. If they have a problem with that you can always threaten their jobs. That will have some punch when they believe you will do it."

Raymond admitted to himself he did not know much about leading people, but this way seemed contrary to what he believed. This arrangement had the potential to make him more dependent upon Mr. Thomas than when he was as a miner – the fact that he lacked knowledge and experience. He knew, initially any way, that he could not make decisions without first consulting Mr. Thomas.

Mr. Thomas continued, "There is one other idea I have that will work to our advantage. Have you ever heard of an air hammer or drill?"

"I think I have heard of them, but I do not have a clue how it works."

"That is fine. I will send you to Wellspring to train you on it." You'll then know how to make their work go quicker and be more productive. They'll depend on your leadership. Knowledge is power."

Mr. Thomas elaborated, "Conventional mining is slow and can only produce so much silver, even when the rocks are prime. We are going to upgrade to a steam-powered air hammer. I want you to leave for Wellspring right after Thanksgiving. Victoria will make the arrangements. Go to The Mercantile and pick out a couple of blue work shirts and new dungarees. You will be representing Thomas Mines and we don't want you looking shabby.

"Finally, I want you to do one more thing, Raymond. Up until you go to Wellspring and after you return, I want you to keep your ears open. Let me know who is grumbling and what they are grumbling about, so we can deal with it."

"Oh, I know one thing they would like. The biggest concern I have heard is they would like more money for their work. I was thinking of a bonus plan in which they could be rewarded for increased production."

"I understand your concerns and I know you have some ideas, but you leave the management to me." Mr. Thomas responded in a serious tone. "I particularly want you to watch for and listen especially of any talk about unions or organizing the workers. Down below, they have the luxury of being able to call out the militia or federal troops. They can claim the mining of coal is of national security and can get assistance in forcing the miners back to work. They can even use soldiers to mine the coal, and that is only after a work stoppage. The owners do not even have to pay for security.

"Up here, we have to call on the Pinkertons. They can 'encourage' workers not to organize and actually have more methods to persuade than the use of troops, since they are not really subject to the law of the land. But they are expensive."

Raymond suddenly felt as if he was being asked to be the classroom tattle tale. Any other ideas or innovations he might have entertained seemed suddenly less significant. So much for idealism or imagining one could actually make a difference through effective leadership. He resolved then and there, whenever he would talk to Mr. Thomas; he would mostly listen and be very reluctant to offer opinion.

"There is one more thing Victoria will discuss with you. I will take a walk and be back in a while."

As Mr. Thomas put his coat and hat on and left the room, Victoria began a conversation. "As you know, Christmas is coming in two months. It is a tradition for the employees to present Father with a gift at the annual Christmas dinner. Mr. Peters was always in charge of the gift in the past. Now you will be responsible to organize the collection, so you might start reminding the miners and getting their ideas as to what they would like to give."

Raymond, attempting to conceal his reaction to the incredulity of the situation, said, "I will get right on that tomorrow. What in the world could your dad want or need?"

Victoria responded, "Oh, it's not the gift that matters. It's the idea of honoring my father for all he does for the miners."

Soon Mr. Thomas returned from his "walk" and Raymond thanked the Thomases again for dinner. He bid them "Good day," and returned to his room. On the way there, in the deserted street, with the autumn sky hanging overhead, he detected traces of winter in the dark clouds. With the afternoon turning to early twilight, and the hints of winter in the air, he felt as if he had been beaten up with nobody even laying a hand upon him.

Chapter Eight

THANKSGIVING

Stewart looked forward to the days when he and Michael would put everyday concerns aside and the two could spend time talking. The fact that neither man had an outside fulltime job did not mean the two could sit and talk as they would have preferred. Michael slept in short intervals. He was on no schedule so he could sleep as he chose. When he could not sleep at night, he could read as many hours as he liked. His lamp was not so bright that it disturbed Stewart's sleep. The room was arranged in such a manner that the two had semi-private areas, as Michael had fashioned a type of partition from animal hides between the bed and the hammock. Stewart also laid his head toward the partition, so he was not facing the light.

Stewart spent most of his time working. He had to prepare for winter and take care of Michael's needs. Stewart had to use the daylight to his advantage, and as winter neared, the number of daylight hours diminished greatly. His initial hope was to spend some extra time in the mountains. This experience surpassed his wildest dreams. He also spent time tanning hides, working with leather and making riggings for his own travel. So far, in addition to the items he made or repaired for Michael, he made a utility sheath for his pocket knife, a "possible" bag or courier to carry his lunch and small items, and a binder like the one Michael used for his writing.

Some evenings, when Michael would take a long nap, if he did not fall asleep himself, Stewart explored Michael's book collection. He knew it would be some time before he would have this many books in one place without having to visit a library. He was very thankful Michael valued books and took the extra efforts to cart them up on Clementine. Inside the front cover was a printed label much like you found in a library book. The printed portion said, "Return this book within two weeks or pay _____. (The blank had penciled in $1.00.) If you damage the book, never ask to borrow another." In cursive was written, at the top of the label, "Michael Thomas."

This morning, Stewart opened the cover of one book by Alfred M. Mayer, entitled, *Sport With Gun and Rod,* dated 1883. There was no label inside this book. In cursive, it simply said, "This book belongs to Michael Thomas. Do not ask to borrow this book." On the page across from the label was an inscription, "To Michael, a good soldier and a man of courage. Your friend, T.R."

Stewart opened the book and began reading a paragraph that had been underlined in pencil:

> The love of the chase is deeply imbedded in man's nature. During the untold centuries of his savage condition he followed it of necessity. We now revert to our primitive employment for our pleasure and recreation, pursuing with ardor, sports which often involve much bodily fatigue and always require skill and training. An impulse, often irresistible it seems, leads a man away from civilization, from its artificial pleasures and its mechanical life, to the forest, the fields, and waters, where he may have that freedom and peace which civilization denies him. If this be not so, then why is it that a man of affairs as well as the man of leisure feels again the joy of his youth as he bids farewell to his office or his club, and seeks the solitudes of the woods and the plains?
>
> He will meet there some old familiar face in a guide, or fellow-sportsman, and welcome it with the ardor of good-fellowship. He will undergo all sorts of bodily discomfort — course food and rough bed, the wet and the cold — and yet be happy, because for a little spell he is free. In other words, he has, for a time, become a civilized savage.

If, with gun and rod, he goes into the recesses of the great woods, and lives there for weeks or months, or mounts his horse and traverses the western plains and mountain passes, relying on his rifle for his sustenance, he is made to realize that there are many things to be learned outside of cities and away from usual occupations.

He will find food for philosophy in the behavior of his hunting companions; he will see who is manly and unselfish, who endowed of his pluck and self-reliance; for three weeks' association with a friend in the wilderness will reveal more of his character than a dozen years with him amid the safe retreats and soothing comforts of civilized life. He will learn how few are the real wants of a happy life in the midst of uncivilized nature. His troubles, if he carried any with him, will vanish; time will seem of as little value to him as to the savage, and like all true sportsmen and "honest anglers," he will return to his home with a calmed spirit and a contented mind.

Stewart closed the book, taking a deep sigh and attempting to drink in everything he had just read. As he reflected the words in relation to his own recent experience, he said, "Amen!"

Michael was beginning to stir from his morning nap. Thanksgiving Day had come and Stewart set the whole day aside so he and Michael could celebrate. "Something sure smells good!"

"It is all ready to go. I was just waiting for you to wake up from your nap."

Stewart served the meal. The two ate quietly and pensively. Michael did not have much of an appetite yet as he did not get any physical activity. Since he finished eating first, he began the conversation. "That was a mighty fine meal."

"Thank you. I never thought I'd get any good at cooking. I'm actually enjoying it. Gramps used to say, 'The things you do to make you happy are not as important as the things in which you choose to be happy.'"

"Sounds about right. What books were you looking at when I woke up?"

"The hunting book. That book describes in a nutshell exactly what I have experienced. Who is T.R.?"

Michael smiled pleasantly as he thought back over the several fond memories. "T.R. is Teddy Roosevelt."

Stewart was stunned for a moment as in disbelief. "How did you know him?"

"I told you I fought in Cuba with T.R."

"Yeah, but I thought you meant you were in Cuba at the same time."

"I was a Rough Rider. He had written his own book by the time of the war, but gave me a personal copy of this book. I have never met anybody like him. His books were *Hunting Tips of a Rancher* and *The Wilderness Hunter*. Let me read two of Teddy's paragraphs. I want to show you something about his beliefs and the difference in his writing style to Mayer's:"

Hunting in the wilderness is of all pastimes the most attractive, and it is doubly so when not carried on merely as a pastime. Shooting over a private game preserve is of course in no way to be compared to it. The wilderness hunter must not only show skill in the use of rifle and also the qualities of hardihood, self-reliance, and surroundings, the fact the hunter needs the game both for its meat and for its hide, undoubtedly adds a zest to the pursuit.

Among the hunts which I have most enjoyed were those made when I was engaged in getting in the winter's stock of meat for the ranch, or was keeping some party of cowboys supplied with game from day to day.

"Here is another selection:

We need, in the interest of the community at large, a rigid system of game laws rigidly enforced, and it is not only admissible, but one may almost say necessary, to establish, under the control of the State, great national forest reserves, which shall also be a breeding grounds and nurseries for wild game; but I should much regret to see grow up in this country a system of large private games preserves, kept for the enjoyment of the very rich. One of the chief attractions of the life of the wilderness is its rugged and stalwart democracy; there every man stands for what he actually is, and show himself to be.

"You see, Mayer talks about the ethereal, the ephemeral, and the philosophy behind hunting. He talks about building relationships. T.R. talks about action, personal challenge, necessity and, of course, "how can we legislate this into being?"

"Yes, I see."

Stewart poured them both some more coffee and settled in for what he hoped was a long story.

"Teddy, ever since he was a young man, loved the outdoors and nature. He always preached and lived the 'rugged life.' He had asthma as a child and believed he cured it by going outdoors, and exerting himself in hiking and hunting. His philosophy was, "Live life one day at a time and live each day to the fullest."

"How did you get into the Rough Riders?"

"Teddy wanted a special group. As Secretary of the Navy, he had latitude other people did not have. Most of us were cowboys, miners, western bad men, eastern dandies and sportsmen. Hamilton Fish was on the Harvard rowing team and a close personal friend of T.R.

In training to go to Cuba and all during the war, if you watched him closely, you would have thought you were involved in a huge sporting event. His slogan was, 'Get action; do things; be sane; don't fritter away time; create; act; take a place wherever you are and be somebody; get action.'

"He offered praise and encouragement all the time. Morale was always high simply because we were serving with him. Most ranking officers, in leading a charge, would say, 'Go up' and lead from behind. He would get in front and say, 'Come up.'

When we were in the heat of battle, he refused to take cover if his men were uncovered. It was a miracle and a huge dose of grace, that he never got shot. It was almost as if he knew destiny was hanging on his head. Remind me later and I will tell you a couple of stories about the war."

Stewart took this opportunity to clear the table after he removed Michael's lap tray and refilled the coffee cups. He helped Michael recline a little in bed so they could talk more easily while Stewart worked. When he finished he got a big boyish grin on his face. "I will be right back," he told Michael.

Michael had a surprised expression as he wondered what Stewart might be up to. Steward came back into the cabin holding something behind his back. "What are you hiding?"

"Only this."

Stewart pulled a crutch from behind his back. He had fashioned it from a limb, hand carved it, and finished it.

"Hey that looks like a good one. Let's try it out!"

"Are you sure you are ready?"

"I had better get on my feet soon. You can't stay around here forever."

Stewart contemplated Michael's statement. He realized he had not really thought much about leaving. He could put contemplation off until some future time. Now he was reminded of how he wanted to go to Wellspring and learn. He was also not sure how soon Michael would be able to walk, or at least get around unassisted.

Stewart took the crutch over to Michael. He held the crutch in one hand and gently but firmly took Michael by the arm. "Are you ready?"

"Yes. I don't think I can't walk yet, but we have to start somewhere."

Stewart worked to swing Michael's legs around to the side of the bed. He placed the crutch under Michael's arm. Slowly, leaning on Stewart, Michael stood on his good leg and balanced himself on the crutch.

"How does it feel?"

"Strange, but I don't plan to be on it forever."

Stewart began walking Michael around the room. "I have been thinking about our conversation we had a few weeks ago – the one about the railroad. I want to build my tracks in this wilderness we call life, but I don't even know where to begin planning."

"That's understandable. You seem to be more focused than I was at your age. We can never really plan the events which we undergo. We have to be in constant preparation so we will be ready when the opportunity presents itself. T.R. always said, 'Keep your powder dry.' He was not talking about war, as we no longer loaded our own muzzles. We used manufactured cartridges. He meant, 'Be prepared. You never know what opportunity will present itself.'

"One year after Teddy graduated from Harvard, he was elected to the new York State Assembly. That is where he became a leader of the GOP as a "Reformer." In those years he wrote several of his books, including the *Navel War of 1812*. In 1884, his wife and mother both died on the same day. He left politics and the public life for a spell to become a rancher in the 'Badlands.'

"He returned to New York in 1886 to run for mayor. He finished third by 60,000 votes. With these setbacks and tragedies he never gave up. In 1895, he wanted to run for mayor again. Edith, his new wife was carrying their fourth child, so she persuaded him not to run. His friend, Henry Cabot Lodge, noticed him sulking around about not running and encouraged him to accept an appointment form Mayor Strong to be New York Police Commissioner. Henry told him he could fight corruption from that level.

"Teddy accepted. He and Jacob Riis, a journalist conducted mid night raids in the lower east side of Manhattan and found unsafe factories and unsanitary conditions in the tenement slums. He experienced the overcrowding of Lower East Side Manhattan. He also fought to clean up corruption in the police force. He and Riis found and exposed 'lazy' cops, fought against corrupt officials and for pay and promotions based upon performance rather than politics.

"He realized it was the battle, public journalism and political persuasion that would change things, not force. That was where he gained the values that later became his national agenda for reform.

"There was something else T.R. gained from his police commissioner days. He had a nostalgic fondness for the Colt 38. There were other, more powerful guns around, but since the police used the Colt, Teddy liked it. The irony was that he carried a Colt in Cuba. It had been issued to the captain of the battle ship Maine. When the Maine exploded in Savanna Harbor, Navy divers recovered it.

"The sinking of the Maine was the single motive most likely responsible to incite public sentiment in favor of invading the Spaniards. Two hundred and sixty men died in the explosion. There was speculation that they did not even blow it up. People said, 'Maybe we did to start the war.' Others said, 'It might have been accidental.'

Michael continued, "I think the best thing to emphasize is life's priorities. T.R. always kept a Bible next to himself, whether in training or in war. One of his favorite passages was one in which the Master was speaking to a group of teachers of the law and religious leaders – the Pharisees. He was warning them about religion as opposed to real-life faith; 'Woe to you scribes and Pharisees, hypocrites! For you tithe mint and dill and cumin, and have neglected the weightier provisions of the law; justice and mercy and faithfulness…'

"You see, just as in those days, there are people who like to use the law for their benefit. They are not necessarily religious leaders, but those who like to control and manipulate others, by force if necessary. They don't understand the difference between power and authority. To them, the end justifies the means."

"What is the difference?"

"Power is the ability to put restraint upon others by force. The force might be the law of the land. It might be Biblical Law – the Ten Commandments, withholding monetary benefits; physical punishment or even the threat of death. Most of those who have the power on their side, for whatever reason espouse the benefits of law and order, and submission to authority.

"These same people are the ones who least desire to be under authority. Authority is not force. It is gained by respect, much like the respect of a child for his mother, or a friend's respect for another friend. Authority is earned. The best leaders are those who lead with authority. They do not have to threaten to get people to follow them. They do not see themselves as being better than the individuals being led, or entitled in any way as if they deserve to be in leadership by birthright. They will not ask anybody to do something they would not do themselves."

"How is respect earned?"

"I can't answer that completely, because it can vary from situation to situation. I can give you an example. On our way back from Cuba, I had a bout of dysentery. T.R. did not need to attempt to impress us. We had won the war and were returning home to a hero's welcome. If I had the strength, I would not have allowed him to do what he did. He took a place in the coach, while he had me placed in his private berth. Even before that, the men would have gladly followed him into hell and back."

"What was so different about him than most leaders?"

"He had self respect. That is how you gain authority. People who have to resort to power to get others to follow them lack respect for themselves. They have to attempt to gain the admiration of others, in a vain attempt to gain self esteem. Respect is earned by trust and gaining the confidence of others. A person who lacks self respect cannot value others. A person who does not trust others can usually not be trusted. They think others are out to get them because of their own warped system of discerning motives.

"Without respect and trust, authority breaks down. When authority breaks down, power takes over. Under the force or power, people are not given any choice in the matter. They are manipulated to do what the one holding the power desires. Authority, in contrast, considers what is best for those under authority. Power does not endure because people eventually overthrow it.

"A simple way to determine if a leader is practicing authority or power is to listen whether the person has a sense of humor. If a person has enough self respect to poke fun at themselves, they are not going to think you are out to overthrow them. If a leader is always serious and defensive, watch out!

Stewart was attempting to soak in every detail of the conversation. He reflectively added, "So, no matter what you are doing, it is best to defend the rights of others, especially those who are not able to defend their own rights, and treat others the way you want to be treated?"

"The principal applies whether you are a king, a president, a parent, an employee or a friend. Always treat people with the utmost respect. You cannot do it if you do not respect yourself."

"Yes, I understand!"

"Treating others as you want to be treated is The Golden Rule. Our society has come to believe another golden rule – he who has the gold, rules.

"There's something else about respect. We can never own people. Sometimes we act as if we could, but if we respect others we have enough confidence in their judgment to allow them to make mistakes. If they fail, we help them pick up the pieces.

"We must continually make people less dependent upon ourselves. Then, if they choose to be with us, it is not because they have to be. If we force people into anything, they will look for ways out, even if they do what is required, they will do it only minimally – their hearts will not be in it.

"So, giving me that crutch is an example of what I am talking about. Nobody has said you have to stay here and help me. You have decided to because you value life and I think you might have some respect for me. I like that. Instead of choosing to be needed, which is a strong motivation for a lot of people; you have attempted to help me stand on my own.

"Eventually, I will put that thing on a mantle with other trophies. I know you well enough to know you will not be hurt when I no longer choose to use your gift. In fact, you will rejoice with me because I have overcome my infirmity. We have shared authority. I have some age on you. You have physical capacity I need. Through mutual respect, we both benefit. We understand and accept our strength and limitations without excuse or regret."

"Michael, I might have saved your life, but you have given me so much life. I feel I am indebted to you," Stewart said with a tear in his eye and a strain in his voice.

"Stewart, you have made this the best Thanksgiving I have ever had. That only reminds me, you never know what life holds in store for you. I was laying on the trail, near dead, just two months ago, and now I have gained the best friend I have ever had."

"So have I."

Chapter Nine

RAYMOND GOES TO WELLSPRING

Raymond was asked to spend Thanksgiving at the Thomases. He would have to leave for Wellspring on Saturday morning on the "Ten-Fifty-Five" in order to be settled in for classes on Monday morning. There would not be much to pack as he only had his old clothes and the new pants and shirts Mr. Thomas told him to purchase. As he folded, unfolded and refolded the clothes, mostly out of nervousness, he thought it curious that he should be present at the Thomas house again.

He listened over and over to the voices in his head – the voices of Mr. Thomas, Victoria and his own - rethinking the logical reasons offered why he was chosen to be foreman. Still, he wondered why he should progress to that position so rapidly.

What might Stewart be doing? Had he found a place in Wellspring? Had he found a job? Would it be difficult to find him? He remembered that his altered plans included catching a train about this time. He thought to himself, "Who knows, if I am able to find Stewart, maybe I'll just write the Thomases a thank note for all they have done and stay in Wellspring as I intended."

He could not admit to himself, although the feeling was at the back of his mind, that he might stay up here forever. He knew it was just a job. What had been offered to him was an excellent opportunity, but he was young enough to believe, with some more schooling, he would probably be able to create positive situations in the future. He knew he would not stay here just for a job.

He was able to admit to himself that the only reason he would stay here was the remotest possibility to win Victoria's heart. He figured the personal aspects would develop. After all, she had to be the one who mentioned to Mr. Thomas that he would be a good candidate for foreman.

As Raymond walked through town, he could see the last visible signs of autumn. There were very few leaves remaining on the aspens. The sky took on a dark gray pallor. A light snow began to fall. Winter was beginning to dominate the scene. He was surprised how much earlier the mountains yielded to the demands of winter than his prairie farm. The unpaved streets in Discovery were muddy and the buildings were dirty.

Back on the farm, the roads or lanes could handle the amount of traffic without getting too muddy, except in the rainy season. They had hauled so much gravel to fill the holes in the drive. Even at that, there was much less concentration of traffic on the farm, and enough space to go a little wider over fresh ground so as to avoid cutting deep ruts.

The buildings had a dust which had been a combination of coal soot, fine wood ash, particles from digging, crushing and blasting. Except for the people and the afternoon sun backlighting the mountains, the town could be depressing. On these autumn days, as soon as the sun began to make shadows a cold chill began to set in. Raymond began to feel the loneliness he so often felt in Discovery. Sure, he liked the other miners, but as hard as he tried to avoid it, his managerial role placed a distance between him and the others.

At work everybody felt the crunch to produce and the despair of working so hard, but never being able to get ahead of the bills. The only times he was able to forget his concerns were when he visited Victoria. That was only true if Mr. Thomas did not attempt to place heavy burdens of guilt on him. The guilt was for being too friendly with the miners, not being serious enough or not pushing them hard enough.

As Raymond approached the Thomas house, a conversation had already begun, "Now Father, I don't want you to talk shop today."

"Well, you know that was the main reason I agreed to invite him over today. I just have one more thing to bring up. Do you think he is totally committed yet?"

"Father, he has taken a major risk to be foreman. He doesn't seem like a risk-taker, but he has accepted a job with a lot of potential for disaster, not to mention that it stretches his personal comfort beyond complacency. "

"And a lot of potential for success!" interjected Mr. Thomas.

"Father, you don't have to sell me on the idea. You know I understand the potential for success in the mines. This can wait until tomorrow at the office. He does not leave until Saturday."

"I know, but I like to kill two birds with one stone. There is not much else to talk about today."

"You could count your blessings."

"Um, we make our own blessings! I just don't want to invest a lot of time and training into someone who can't commit. I think being sent for training will bring him on full bore. I am reluctant to have an employee know about an aspect of mining with which I am unfamiliar. He could get too independent. If I had time I'd go, too."

"Father, you know your organization can only grow if you allow it to grow beyond your own abilities and power. You have to entrust real responsibilities to others."

"I tried that once with my brother. How did that turn out?"

Ring. Ring.

"We can talk more about that later. That's him! No shop talk!"

After Raymond came in, hung his coat and greeted the Thomases, the talk was mostly awkward small talk. Raymond always attempted, especially in the presence of Mr. Thomas, to appear to be totally engaged in the conversation. He always attempted to convince himself and whoever was present that he was not totally interested in whatever Victoria was doing – that he was ever eager to catch a glimpse of her or listen intently when she talked. It became increasingly evident he was fighting a losing battle. He was less aware of his failed attempts than any other observer.

The only thing Mr. Thomas intended to discuss regarding business was that he had heard good reports about Raymond. Raymond, for the most part, felt somewhat comfortable around Mr. Thomas, except when he was in one of his bothersome, cantankerous moods. Mr. Thomas was usually careful not to demonstrate these moods on holidays and weekends.

Raymond liked to be around Victoria, but he, at times probably felt less comfortable around her than he did being around Mr.

Thomas. She held his emotions captive. If she knew the power she had over him, she could have destroyed him at will – if she were of that disposition. Raymond believed Mr. Thomas might have been of that disposition, but he did not have any power over Raymond other than to take his job. Victoria had the power to steal his heart.

He was glad she did not know, at least, she did not appear to him that she knew or even cared what Raymond felt about her. But then, how could she know he was interested? Well, maybe she did not know. Ever since the first meeting, he could not fully compose himself around her. Maybe she did know! That was terrifying! Maybe she was just waiting for the right moment to embarrass him or break his heart. By contrast to his logical thoughts, his inner thoughts still told him he could trust her.

"Did you hear what I said?"

"I am sorry, sir. I was just thinking about what you said." Raymond fumbled to stall, hoping Mr. Thomas would pick up on the conversation where he had drifted out.

"So, you like fishing for compliments, eh? I was saying that I was hearing good reports about you."

"Thank you, sir. I hope I am earning the men's respect."

"Um, well, yes. Of course they respect you. I think maybe, they may even fear you. They know you can recommend disciplinary actions or even dismissal for me to consider. I am sure they don't want to be singled out. A little fear is healthy. You will have an advantage when you have knowledge in an area they don't have. That way they'll depend on you more. Knowledge is power! Oh, and be careful about complimenting too much. They'll get a big head."

Victoria brought some food into the dining room. She looked at Mr. Thomas with her head tilted forward and a frown, as she looked through her brow – noticed by Mr. Thomas, yet unperceived by Raymond. Mr. Thomas understood the gesture. "I guess that is enough shop talk. It looks like dinner is about ready."

During dinner Victoria seemed to be more polite than usual. She looked Raymond in the eye more deeply and seemed to hold her glances longer when he gazed back at her. Could it be that she might be interested in him, too? There were not many single men in town. She certainly would not be allowed to be attracted to a miner, except for the remote possibility of one who was management. None of them had any education or liked to read. At least they had no time or energy to read after a full day at the mines. Maybe there was a basis for mutual attraction. Raymond could only hope.

"Victoria, I've never heard you mention a fiancé or a boyfriend." Raymond almost felt shocked at himself for finding the courage to utter such a bold inquiry. Mr. Thomas looked up from his eating, glancing, unnoticed, at the two people engaged in the conversation.

"Oh, there has been no one of interest to me here and I have been too busy to really think about such a consideration."

She commented as if it was the first time she had thought of such an arrangement. After she said this, she gave a glance that conveyed more warmth then he had ever seen from her. Maybe he will always be in Discovery.

Saturday rolled around. Raymond was up early packing and repacking. He could not sleep from the excitement. Today would be his first train trip. He thought how his clothes took so little room in the leather suit case Mr. Thomas had loaned him. He thought, "How could I get this back to him if I choose to stay in Wellspring?"

He grabbed the suitcase and headed toward the dining room. He could eat a leisurely breakfast, stop by the office for his paperwork, and walk the two blocks to the depot with plenty of time to spare. As he entered the dining room, he noticed himself looking in the direction of the private dining area. Disappointedly, he acknowledged, "They must be at work already. I'm glad I have to stop by the mine office on my way."

Raymond ordered breakfast and drank his coffee. He was excited about the trip and the training, but reluctant about entering Wellspring by himself. The weighty cloud of indecision still hung heavy over him. Because of the extra burden he placed upon himself, some of the excitement of the trip was dampened somewhat.

He finished breakfast and casually walked to the mining office. As he entered the door, he saw Victoria at her desk. She looked up, handed him an envelope and said, "Oh Raymond, here is your expense money. You will have cash for every day needs. Keep receipts. The check goes to the Institute as you register. Your train tickets are there, too. You can keep it all in that leather courier."

"Thank you."

"And Raymond…" He loved to hear the way she pronounced his name and the way she always did so when talking to him. She reached down beside her desk and hoisted a medium-sized flat box. "I couldn't help but notice your work coat at our house. You can't go to Wellspring wearing that old thing."

He opened the box and took out a new denim work coat. "Wow, this is too much. How could I ever repay this?"

"You don't 'repay' gifts. I got it myself."

Raymond walked toward her and wanted to kiss her, at least give her an affectionate hug, but awkwardly reached out his hand to shake hers in a professional manner. Victoria, perceiving the awkwardness, said, "Oh, give me a hug."

"Thank you. I will miss, um…Discovery."

"It's only two weeks. Now go down there and learn all you can. I know you'll do us proud."

As Raymond walked toward the depot, he could actually not remember if his feet hit the ground. He might have been on Cloud Nine. As he neared the depot, he could see the black column of smoke and the smell the coal and wood burning in the boiler of the locomotive, as the train came clanking into the station. The train was idling, coasting and giving off a deep hiss of excess steam every now and then. The snorting reminded Raymond of an angry bull as he pawed the ground. The train rolled to a stop with the screech of metal rubbing metal.

He showed his ticket to the conductor, who seemed preoccupied as he studied his pocket watch and said, "Ten fifty-five," with a smile. He stowed the wooden step in the stair well of the train and shouted toward the engine, "All aboard."

As the train began to roll Raymond stowed his suitcase in the overhead rack and settled in to get comfortable for the six hour ride. As he glanced back toward the direction of the mining office, standing in the alley was Victoria waving goodbye and smiling. His heart leaped in his chest as he waved back.

After waving, he noticed a gentleman sitting in the seat across and facing his. The man wore a dark wool suit with a tie of smooth texture and a floral design. The tie might have been silk, but Raymond would not have known since he had never seen a silk tie.

Raymond also noticed a watch draped from the man's vest pocket to a loop on the vest. Raymond thought back to how his father's watch was worn in his "fifth" pocket of his dungarees as he never had a vest to wear and display his watch chain. Besides that, his fathers' watch was adorned with a braided leather strand rather than a gold chain.

Finally, the train was progressing beyond the Discovery town limits and proceeding down the mountain pass. Raymond stared out the window. The gentleman across from him began a conversation. "So, you're going to Wellspring. Ever been there before?"

"No. This is my first train trip. I have never been this far west."

"So, you're going down for some training? You mean Old Thomas is going to release some money to improve a mining process, and he is not the one going for training?"

Raymond was taken off guard. He was surprised to hear someone call Mr. Thomas anything other than Mr. Thomas. He also wondered how this stranger knew his plans. It was almost as if he were showing off that he knew something about Raymond, while Raymond had no inclination who he might be. Raymond also wondered if it might be a test to see if he would defend Mr. Thomas or eventually report back to him.

"Oh, I'm sorry. Forgive my lack of manners. I'm Robert Conner. I work with old Ned."

Raymond had never heard anybody call Mr. Thomas "Ned" before. Raymond said, "Weren't you at breakfast in the inn this morning? You don't live in Discovery do you? What do you do for the mines?"

"Whoa, I object," said Mr. Conner, jokingly to ease Raymond's tension. "In court, I only have to handle one question at a time, and I usually ask the questions. I am chief prosecuting attorney in Wellspring. Before I became prosecutor, I was with Adams, Bailey and Conner. It is pretty bad when your name begins with a "C" and you are still listed last among the partners."

Raymond looked a little puzzled. This guy could talk.

"I represent Thomas Mines, mostly on mineral rights and mining claims. I'm also an investor and general trouble shooter. It used to be easy. A miner simply staked a workable claim and the square footage was his. As miners began to tunnel deeper into the hills, adjacent boundaries had to be determined including the imaginary vertical division between the claims.

"Then the miners wanted to organize. They have even revolted, held strikes and caused riots in the coal mines. So now I have to keep up on who the organizers are and where they are working. We've been able to keep them out of Discovery, because there's nothing else up here for them.

"They stand out in the community. The only way they can work is to get a job and infiltrate the mine, working from inside. So, I also have to keep contact with the Pinkertons, just in case. When you need them, there's no time to locate them and get them moving. You need them on the next train up."

Raymond had never experienced anything like this conversation. He began to feel as if Mr. Conner was watching his reactions to determine if he was with the Thomases or a possible infiltrator. Raymond could not define it, but he had a strange feeling the jovial multi-directional conversation was a professional, practiced means of lowering a person's defenses to obtain more information and observe reactions. No doubt, it was second nature for a man in Mr. Conner's position. Was it a coincidence that he was on this train, sitting directly across from Raymond and engaging in a conversation?

Raymond decided to talk about what was really on his mind and change the subject. "Have you met Miss Victoria?"

"Oh yes. She is a fine young lady. Anybody of her stature who can deal with the old man surely has pluck."

"I've never seen such an amazing creature as her."

"Boy, you've got it bad. I think your condition might be fatal."

Raymond, a little embarrassed that he could so easily and obviously reveal his condition to a total stranger, acknowledged, "Possibly. Possibly."

To once again ease the tension, since his first tack did not work, Raymond offered, "I'm going to the Mining Institute. Mr. Thomas wants me to learn about the use of steam for drilling and hammering."

Conner burst out again, "Old Thomas is going to finally get the mines into the Steam Age."

Raymond, smiling with a puzzled look, acknowledged the statement with a forced smile. Conner smiled back with a smile that revealed he must have been proud of his observation. "It sounds as if you are moving right into Thomas Mines. This doesn't have anything to do with Miss Victoria, does it?"

Now Raymond grinned as he knew more than he was saying about the subject, but said nothing. Conner continued, "The man who ends up with her will be very lucky and very unfortunate. She'll be a wonderful catch, but I'm afraid her old man will be a package deal for a while. One would certainly find it challenging, at best, to be his son-in-law."

Raymond just smiled dreamily as he shook his head at the thought. Although Raymond might have thought to the contrary, he had only seen Mr. Thomas on his best behavior to this point. There would be time in the not-too-distant future, when he, like everybody else who had been around long enough, would see the other side of Mr. Thomas. The two passengers continued in small talk for a while. Conner took a sip from his pocket flask and offered one to Raymond. Raymond gracefully declined. Pretty soon, Conner drifted off to sleep.

Raymond was happy for the opportunity to take in the scenery. He had never seen such high bridges through the mountain passes. The first two times they crossed a trestle, he held his breath as he could see nothing below the train to suspend it in what appeared to be mid-air. He pulled some lunch that he brought from the inn and had placed in the leather courier.

Most of the spur lines at this time did not yet have dining cars. Raymond continued to watch out the window for the afternoon, listening to the gentle and rhythmic clatter of the wheels hitting the expansion joints on the track. He also enjoyed the gentle side to side swaying of the train as it reached its top speed of about twenty miles for every hour traveled.

Dusk came early and he watched as the sun going over the mountains cast a brilliant violet hue. After sundown, the porter lit a lamp near Raymond's seat, so he began to read. He dozed off for a while. He woke as the train began a downward slope and changed the rhythm of clattering which had lulled him to sleep. As he awoke, he looked to the southwest as the train began to go down a grade of what seemed to be the steepest descent of the day.

There in the distance, the heavy sky of late autumn reflected the lights of Wellspring. He could not pull himself away from the window as he watched. He could see the town drawing nearer and beginning to take a definite shape as the train descended down the switch-backs. For a while the town would be on the right and then the train turned to the other side onto a new switch-back going in the other direction. Then Wellspring would be to his left.

The train continued until they proceeded through tent towns, in which the tents had wooden bases and a canvas top. The streets were in random order, of maybe disorder. Whenever possible, planks were placed to offer make-shift sidewalks. They soon began to pass through areas which appeared to be recently constructed wood frame houses, office buildings, stores, hotels and saloons. The only establishments that appeared as if they were still open for business were the saloons. Occasionally, a hotel would have the foyer lights on. He began hoping there would be a hotel near the depot once he arrived in town, as he did not have a reservation until Sunday night.

He was amazed how quickly the train passed through town. He watched as any pedestrians or horse drawn carriages had to wait for the train to cross the streets. They were now passing mostly brick buildings that looked as if they had been standing for years. He figured this was the center of the city. Soon, the conductor said, "Next stop, Wellspring."

As the train screeched to a stop, Raymond gathered his things, said, "Good-by, it was nice to meet you," to Mr. Conner and shook his hand. He followed the other passengers from the train to the depot and out into the street. There, across the street was a hotel with what appeared to be a casino in the lobby. The place was as busy as mid-day. Reluctantly, Raymond entered the Golden Nugget and asked for a room. By now he was worn out and did not want to look for a quieter setting. The clerk asked if he just wanted a room or anything else. Raymond, with a puzzled look said, "No, just a room."

Sunday morning came and Raymond was up early. He had some important things to accomplish. He had to find out how to get to the Institute and find his hotel in which Victoria had booked a room. He did not know how long they would hold his room and he did not want to have to find a room further from the Institute.

Secondly, he wanted to retrace his steps through town. When he and Stewart agreed to meet at the "edge" of town; did they mean the new shanties in Tent Town; the newly constructed boarding houses and commerce in the wood frame area; or the established brick and mortar central city?

He figured his best bet would be to go the greatest distance in which he could perceive the visible signs of the trail, as it would be obscured by buildings, trees or foothills. He almost wished he could have come in to town by the light of day. That way he would know what the trail looked like coming through the pass with visibility from the train. These were details they could never have foreseen in their planning.

He obtained directions from the desk clerk at the hotel and set out. As he started in an eastward direction, he found an interesting restaurant to get some breakfast. After eating, as he was walking, he noticed the trolley cars proceeding down the tracks in the middle of the street.

After asking for directions, Raymond found himself seated comfortably aboard one of the cars, heading in the general direction of the Mining Institute. As he rode across town, he drank in all the sights and attempted to keep his bearing, so he would later be able to get around on his own. After finding the Institute he checked into his hotel and placed his things in the room.

The next plan was to travel back across toward the trail head and begin to look around town in an effort to locate Stewart. Raymond rode the trolley back to the end of the line. Then he walked several blocks. After an hour's walk, he reached an area in which the wood frame buildings began to be outnumbered by tents. He visited several stores and hotels.

At the establishments that had notes and cards on make-shift bulletin boards, he left notes to Stewart. The bulletin boards had a wide variety of notes on them, some fresh and others were so old the writing had long since weathered off. People did not bother taking the old ones down, they just pinned or tacked new ones over the old. After asking around to gather any information about Stewart or where a young man might go to in town, he started back to his hotel.

Raymond enjoyed the opportunity to learn at the Institute. The two weeks flew by. As Raymond spent his last night in town he reflected back on the trip. He thought Mr. Thomas would be impressed, if not a little threatened by what he had learned. It made him feel a sense of satisfaction that a man who had gained all that Mr. Thomas had gained, might be a little intimidated by him – at least by his newly acquired knowledge.

He also wondered if Victoria would be proud of him and if she would tell him if she was proud. Finally, he thought the men might respect him, or at least respect his newly acquired knowledge. Even though he had not found Stewart, he considered it a good trip.

Chapter Ten

MID-WINTER

Christmas Eve came to Discovery. The winter was fairly mild, for winter in the mountains. There was about a foot of snow on the ground in places where it accumulated without being cleared. Some of the newly fallen snow hid the coal soot and airborne wood ash that rolled from the home chimneys and the smelter.

The miners were in good spirits as they reported for work. They knew they would only work a half day today and not very hard at that. They also knew this would be the one night Edward Thomas would feed them and not charge any of his silver tokens.

At noon, Raymond pulled the long blast on the whistle to indicate the end of the work day rather than the shorter noon whistle he normally blew. It seemed to him as if most of the men cleared the mine before the end of the whistle blast. As the miners passed, tugging on their coats and hats, Raymond said, "Merry Christmas, see you at the dinner tonight."

Several answered with variations to the same theme, "You better believe we'll be there."

Raymond arrived at the Silver Horseshoe, which was closed early; to help move tables around so there would be room for the party. They also kept a little space open so couples could dance after dinner to the music of the local musicians. This was the only night of the year most of them were able to celebrate collectively.

They could usually not afford to hang around the saloon or were simply too tired from work. Most of the family men could not justify visiting the saloon even if they did not imbibe. Tonight, the Silver Horseshoe was not a saloon. It was a place of celebration for families and friends.

As the guests started to arrive, most brought something they could share, a pie, a plate of cookies, or maybe some nut bread. Mr. Thomas had informed them he would provide the meat and vegetables. He also offered free alcohol, but encouraged the miners to only drink in moderation. A couple of men who liked to show off their hunting skills brought fresh game they shot that afternoon.

The atmosphere was quite congenial during the dinner. After everyone had time to eat, get seconds and visit the dessert table, Victoria signaled Raymond to announce the presentation portion of the party. During this segment, Mr. Thomas gave his remarks, congratulated people, gave the Christmas bonus tokens and received his present from all the workers. He always managed to act surprised as the gift was given and words of exaltation were bestowed upon him. In several of the private conversations around the room, more remarks were exchanged:

"I don't know why he acts so surprised, the contributions for the gift are mandatory."

"Yeah, and besides we buy it from his store. He actually makes a profit from the sale."

Out of hearing distance from the previous conversation someone said, "It's getting very difficult to think of something to buy."

"I know, he already has everything."

Mr. Thomas was thinking something else. His thoughts were, "I really don't need this stuff, but I am so glad they show their true respect. They must really think I am a great leader and provider."

As the evening wore down, families with young children began filtering out so they could get home and put the young ones to bed. Some of the couples, with no children or with children old enough to take care of themselves, stayed to dance. Raymond found himself dancing almost every dance with Victoria. They could tell most of the eyes in the room were glued to them - especially the eyes of Mr. Thomas.

Some more conversations could be heard in various places around the room:

"I think something's beginning to develop there, don't you?"

"I think it's quite obvious."

"I wonder how long it'll take Victoria to break that young colt."

"She already has. I wonder how long it'll take Mr. T. to break him."

Finally, only one couple remained besides Raymond and Victoria. "It's getting late. May I see you home?"

"I'd be delighted. I didn't even notice Father leaving."

On the way to the Thomas house, Raymond noticed Victoria had a glove only on one hand - the hand further from him. He gently reached for her bare hand and said, "This might get cold."

"I think it'll be protected."

"Victoria, there's something I want to tell you, but I don't want to tell your dad."

"I guess, but I don't know why you wouldn't want me to tell him. I tell him everything."

"This pertains to work. I'm afraid he might misconstrue my thoughts. I really don't know if I'm cut out for what I'm doing."

"Oh, it's natural to have doubts about your new job. My father will go a long way letting a person learn the job, if you confide in him and he feels you're totally committed to the mines and to... him," she responded in an attempt to encourage him.

By this time, they were standing in front of the door, and paused a moment to finish the conversation. I mean I am not sure I will be happy doing this forever."

"If you stick with it, you have a chance to become very wealthy."

"I know, but I don't know if I'll be happy."

"Oh Raymond, you just lack direction. You don't know what you want out of life," Victoria replied, beginning to demonstrate a certain level of exasperation.

"I know what I want, but money isn't part of it."

"Raymond, you have to set your sights upon professional accomplishments too. Money isn't everything, but it can sure release you from some of the burdens of life to enjoy the things you like."

"Victoria, your dad knows exactly what he wants and would do anything to achieve it. I just don't know if it's worth it."

"Raymond, I'm not sure I know exactly what you mean, but please take my advice and never speak ill of my father."

The sharp rebuke stung Raymond like a slap across the cold cheek. He told Victoria, "Good night," and was on his way. He had hoped this would be the night he gave her his first kiss, but was not as sure as he had previously been regarding where he stood with her.

The two interlopers did not realize the latter part of their conversation was overheard by Mr. Thomas. He waited up and could overhear Raymond's concerns very clearly from his seat between the door and the window. He thought, "Good going, Victoria, thank you for the defense."

He also thought, "As long as Raymond confronts my daughter instead of me, I have him right where I want him. If he has no dreams, I'll give him mine."

"Um, uhg, Is that you Victoria? I must have fallen asleep while I was waiting for you."

Raymond had unwittingly become a greater challenge for Mr. Thomas. He was not calculating, but the amount of reluctance he demonstrated, became a goal for Mr. Thomas to overcome. After all, what could this young man know about leadership that he could not himself demonstrate?

Raymond was invited to the Thomas' for Christmas dinner. As he was getting ready to go, he could think of no other place where he would rather spend Christmas, or any other day for that matter. In spite of Mr. Thomas' ominous presence, Raymond enjoyed time there very much.

He spent most of his morning eating breakfast at the inn and sitting in the dining room reading and drinking coffee. He noticed that Sarah was serving in fancier cups than usual. She also poured the coffee from a pot that had a matching bear design on it. She kept them on the wood stove that was used to heat the dining room and keep food warm between servings.

All the flatware and serving dishes were nicer today than the usual daily wear. They were still in no way as nice as the everyday items found in the Thomas alcove. Raymond wondered if Sarah had to request the holiday ware, although Mr. Thomas did seem more sentimental than usual during the holiday season.

Raymond did not want to be alone for any part of the day. He thought about home and the family. He wondered what they would have for dinner, what his sister had received for a gift, what Mom and Dad bought or made for each other.

He returned, in his mind, to his favorite subject of thought. Victoria could cook like no other woman he had ever met. Sure

Mom was a great cook, but being on the farm, she was more of a meat and potatoes cook. The food prepared by Victoria was the best one could obtain in the winter. Mom had canned all vegetables the previous summer for their winter provisions. Whether they were in the mountains or on the family farm, he knew the food up here cost a lot, but it was sure worth it. He tried to estimate how much it cost to ship canned vegetables and fresh or processed fruit by rail to this remote area.

Of course, the taste and aroma of the food was secondary to Victoria's company. He thought how his affection seemed to be reciprocated. Then, he wondered if the sharp rebuke from the previous night might overshadow the day. After all, he trusted her and had no basis from which to form an opinion since he had never been in a situation like this before. He wondered if anybody else had felt this certain and confused at the same time before.

Raymond figured the food and spending time with Victoria was worth putting up with Mr. Thomas. He always stressed his point in conversation and had a need to be right, even if the point was hardly worth arguing. An example was the previous Sunday when Raymond had casually mentioned something about Lincoln being born in Kentucky. Mr. Thomas began to argue a little combatively, as if sparring for sport. Raymond said, "With all due respect, I believe we could look it up."

Mr. Thomas had become irritable. Raymond, with stern glances from Victoria, as tactfully as possible, changed the subject. Mr. Thomas later interjected into the conversation of Raymond's confusion about the states. At first, Raymond thought it a trifle and shook it off. Later, he seemed troubled by the vindictiveness and the need to be right exhibited by Mr. Thomas.

No matter, this was Christmas day and Raymond was spending it with Victoria. He finished his coffee, went back upstairs, put his book away, splashed some water on his face and took a last look in the mirror. He strolled over to the house, whistling.

They had a wonderful dinner, as usual. After dinner, they exchanged gifts. Mr. Thomas seemed more preoccupied than usual and shortly excused himself. "Where does he go when he leaves?"

"One time I asked him. He reminded me his job was to watch over me and we should not get the roles reversed. I've heard he goes to the saloon to play cards with some people visiting town."

"Who would be visiting on Christmas Day?"

"I don't know," she said abruptly.

Raymond remembered back to meeting Mr. Conner on the train, but he did not want to mention to Victoria they had met. Raymond knew better than to dig too deeply into the topic, so he changed the subject. "You're so different than any of the town people. In fact, I have never met anybody like you. Where did you get your fascination for books?"

"I lived with my Aunt Whitney for a time. My mom died after she came to Discovery. Father built a big new house for her, but the flu came through and she did not make it through the winter. He kept me in private school and thought I would be in better care if I stayed with Mom's sister, at least for a while. When I left on the train, he never thought it would be four years.

"Before he came here, he and my Uncle Michael tried everything, but could not keep the farm. Father decided to stake a claim and prospect. Amazingly, he struck it rich, unlike so many others who failed and returned home, broke. He was only making enough to support one person, at first.

He sent for Michael and they agreed to be partners. Michael built the smelter and they began to prosper. He started to get the town established and sent for Mom and me when the railroad finished its spur line into Discovery. Michael was gone to war for a short time. During that time my mother died, and I was sent off to Aunt Whitney's.

"Whenever I would object about his working the others too hard, taking short cuts on safety, or using placer mining after it had been banned, he would say, 'Oh, she got her liberal views from her crazy aunt and her big city education.'

"What happened to placer mining?"

"It was outlawed in the Mining Act of 1872. The process destroyed too much of the natural environment, caused erosion, and pollution. He argued that it was more economical and why should he be punished in his ability to make money?

"I prefer to think I was influenced more by the stories my Uncle Michael used to tell me. My favorite was the story of Moses. When he was born he was sentenced to death along with all the other Israelite boys up to two years old. Pharaoh had become concerned that the Hebrew slaves were prospering even though he had done everything possible to prevent them from flourishing. The irony was that Moses was raised in the very house of Pharaoh by his own mother as a maid-servant.

"He became the second most powerful man in the most powerful nation on earth. He even found more favor and earned more responsibility than Pharaoh's own son. Later, he saw an Egyptian abusing an Israelite. He acted impulsively and slew the Egyptian. He had to flee for his life, because he stood against injustice, even though he went too far. He lived in exile for forty years. In a moment, he chose between the wealth, comfort, privilege and prosperity of Egypt to live in exile as a shepherd."

"What about your Uncle Michael? What happened to him?"

Victoria's countenance became very sober. "He stole a load of silver from Father and never came back to town."

"Why?"

"I don't know. Maybe he got desperate. I try to remember him before that happened, and believe something happened to cause him to act in a way he wouldn't have acted under normal circumstances. I hope he comes back someday and asks for Father's forgiveness. I know Father is big enough to forgive him."

Raymond was staring into Victoria's eyes. Something about the vulnerable look that thinking and talking about Michael and the past made her irresistible. He leaned closer. She did not turn her head or pull away. The first kiss.

Christmas had come and gone. The day was like most other days spent in the cabin. Stewart realized when he was staying with Michael, Christmas had not been just another day. Rather, most days were like Christmas. They had friendship, a warm cabin with plenty of firewood and food laid away. Stewart only hoped he was giving, at least in part, back to Michael. He knew Michael had taught and drawn wisdom from him. He wondered what he was giving Michael.

They had both dozed off while sitting by the fire in the late afternoon. Stewart woke first, stirred the fire and made some more coffee. His rustling caused Michael to stir. Stewart filled the cups when the coffee was ready. As they warmed themselves they began to converse. Michael began a topic he had only mentioned once prior to this afternoon. He only mentioned it previously due to Stewart's prodding. The topic was the past, in Discovery. Michael asked, "Have you ever despaired of life?"

Stewart answered, "I think I might have an idea of what you mean, but I am not sure."

"I guess I would ask, 'Have you ever just felt like giving up?' I did in Discovery. I had seen the dreams of youth die. I had always hoped to farm the family land with my brother. Then our parents died so suddenly. We held on longer than we should have until it was all gone. We weren't even able to sell the land. That didn't do it, though.

It seems the disasters which were brought upon us and were beyond our control made us stronger. Or it could be we were so young and foolish we thought we could handle anything.

"It seemed more like the chain of events which kept happening tended to finally wear us down. We tended to grieve more over choices which turned bad than over natural disaster. For example, try taking a person's life and he will fight you, but a person can give up and might even consider taking his own life. Some people call it melancholy. I call it the 'Despondency.'

"Sometimes you wake from a deep sleep and start thinking. You don't want to think, but you do. You just want to go back to sleep. You think of things that need to get done. You haven't put them off, but for everything you get done, you feel like there are two more in its place. You think of things you could have done and things you wish you hadn't done. The harder you fight to sleep, the more you find yourself wide awake.

"Then, you get the dreaded realization that you are getting older. The things that used to be easy, like going through the day with little sleep, or putting in a full day's work with energy to spare, become more difficult. When you are doing your required daily tasks, you want to be sleeping. When you are in bed, trying to go sleep, you wish it were day so you could get things done. The night seems endless and the things you picture in your mind seem to have a dark pallor of dread hanging over them.

"To top it all off, there is one thing worse than not having dreams or not reaching the dreams you have. That is spending all your efforts on one thing and then accomplishing it to find it wasn't really what you wanted at all."

Stewart inquired, "It almost sounds as if nothing is worth the effort."

"Not at all! The best object of life is to put the most effort into everything. Do the best you can at what you have and then as you accomplish it, move on to the next thing. As you get older, you hope you find the time to rest physically, but you have to guard your thoughts. You have to focus on the positive and learn to appreciate each day. This is what Psalm ninety talks about in learning to number our days that we may be found with a heart of wisdom.

"Let me show you those verses," said Michael, as he fumbled for his Bible.

"Psalm ninety, twelve to seventeen says,

Teach us to number our days aright, that we may gain a heart of wisdom. Relent, O Lord! How long will it be? Have compassion on your servants. Satisfy us in the morning with your unfailing love, that we may sing for joy and be glad all our days, Make us glad for as many days as you have afflicted us, for as many years as we have seen trouble. May your deeds be shown to your servants. Your splendor shown to their children. May the favor of the Lord our God rest upon us; establish the work of our hands for us - yes, establish the work of our hands.

"Then, over in ninety-one, five through eight, he says: 'You will not fear the terror of the night, nor the arrow that flies by day, nor the pestilence that stalks in the darkness, nor the plague that destroys at midday. A thousand may fall at your side; ten thousand at your right hand, but it will not come near you. You will only observe with your eye and see the punishment of the wicked.'

"That sure sounds like San Juan Hill. Teddy and all of us displayed this type of courage. Do you know that most of the terrors you imagine are worse than the actual incidents themselves? San Juan Hill was worse, but we showed courage.

One other verse related to these that you need to know to equip yourself. Proverbs five, one and two says, 'My son, pay attention to My wisdom, listen well to My words of insight, that you may maintain discretion and your lips may preserve knowledge.'

"Some translations say, 'Discernment,' in place of 'discretion.' Now if you number your days, live each day to the fullest, and one day at a time, you will have discernment and discretion. You will be able to understand people's motives and not find yourself hoodwinked by them. You will not worry over things that you can do nothing about anyway, you will find joy, and God will confirm the works of your hands.

Stewart asked, "Michael, what have you done since you have been up here?"

"A lot of thinking. The main conclusion I have drawn is the only things of lasting value, besides the necessities of survival, are those things which affect the lives of others. Those things which cause others to evaluate their perspectives and change them as needed."

"It's kind of ironic, Michael. You charged up San Juan Hill in Cuba, but you retreated into the San Juan Mountains when you came here."

"I guess that is correct. I never thought of that."

"You know, my brother had a certain passion for life. He used to say he made his own way and if you worked hard, you will be successful. That was true to a degree. He did not account for God's grace. God provides for the sparrows, but they still have to gather. The part my brother didn't understand is that God provided. His passion was for what he could accomplish or acquire. I don't think he ever thought about the wisdom of seeking God's will for his life. His was a sense of entitlement, as if to say, 'Success is owed to me.'

"He thought we were successful because of his ability to select where to dig and our hard work. He failed to take into account that he stumbled onto the site where Discovery is located. We were also quite fortunate that prospectors were going through and needed supplies. We were able to make some money and offer a service by opening the wood-fired smelter. He must have had some political pull in obtaining the spur line into town and obtaining an investor. That opened everything. He could then ship the silver out, obtain coal to upgrade his smelter and obtain supplies to resell.

"Another irony was that my brother thought any government intervention was wrong as it hindered his ability to make a fortune, such as child labor laws, anti-trust legislation, women's suffrage, and pollution restrictions. He did, however want government guarantees to purchase silver to mint coins, and protection and security. He wanted the benefits of free enterprise without the liabilities or responsibilities.

Stewart added, "Following that line of logic, he was probably in favor of slavery, as it helped those with the means to maintain their high standard of living with cheap or free labor."

"We did not talk about slavery. We were both too young to fight in the Civil War."

They continued to talk long into the night. Finally, Stewart felt so tired he had to excuse himself to go to bed. As he turned in, he noticed Michael was sitting at the table with a lamp, writing intensely. Stewart quickly drifted off into a deep sleep.

Morning arrived very quickly. It seemed he had just closed his eyes on the silhouette of Michael writing at the table, to open them again to find the cabin dark. He realized he had slept the night away and it was now early morning.

He decided to get up and tend to the stove, make some coffee and start breakfast. As he lit the lamp, he noticed some notes scribbled on a paper. Trying not to be too nosey, he started to arrange the papers into a neat stack so they would require less room on the table. He looked at a page which read: "When I hear a heart-felt performance or read an inspiring thought, I sometimes weep - not only because the music was beautiful or the thought deeply profound. Rather, I weep when I see someone applying themselves and putting their heart into their expression, demonstrating passion. Though they may never obtain it, they are reaching for their potential."

Stewart wept too because he discerned the heart of the man who wrote these thoughts. He understood what it meant to display passion in your expression.

Chapter Eleven

THE DEPARTURE

Stewart knew the time for his departure was drawing near. He viewed the possibility with very mixed emotions. He hated the thought of leaving Michael and not being around his enriching but simple environment. He looked forward, however, with increasing anticipation to moving on with his life. When he decided to venture through the mountains into Wellspring, he knew there would be many possibilities.

Stewart knew, upon leaving home, that he would probably find a career, meet the best friend of his life and, yes, probably find a wife. He had no idea he would meet such a good friend as Michael, this short of a distance into the mountains. He was particularly surprised to find such a good friend with so much difference in age and experience from his own.

While he was thinking, Michael got out of bed, assisted by his crutch, and walked over to the table. He had a distinct limp, yet was beginning to get around the cabin without assistance." Michael, are you going to be able to hunt and fend for yourself when I leave?"

"Of course, boy. Don't worry about an old man like me. Shoot, I'm all rested and ready to wrestle a bear."

"Michael, I wasn't trying to be nosey, but I noticed some of the material you have written. I think it's wonderful!"

"I thought it might be useful for me to keep my thoughts recorded. Writing helps me sort out my experiences and find some consolation for having gone through so many of them. Who knows, somebody else might be able to read through it and get something."

"It seems you have so much to share. I know people will find it useful. If someone could suffer a little less by reading about your suffering, it'll have been worth the effort. If somebody gains by reading about the injustices you suffered, that may bring some sort of restitution and healing."

"Well. I hope so. If someone could suffer a little less by reading about my suffering, I suppose the second sacrifice of writing it down is worth the effort. It is kind of like the firewood analogy we discussed earlier. You get warmed when you cut it, and increase your strength and stamina, due to the physical effort. Then the person with whom you share the fire and you both get warmed. I don't think we go through any of life's experiences without a purpose. I know I could not write about justice if I hadn't experienced injustice."

"I know what you mean. I look forward to reading your work."

"Stewart, you have been a great inspiration to me. You saved my life, but more importantly you have helped regain my perspective."

Michael thought for a moment and continued, "You know an injury to our soul is much like an injury to our body. First, it takes time to get over the initial hurt. During that time you have trouble believing somebody could actually treat you in such a way. You feel like you have an open wound. Just like a physical injury immobilizes a person, an injury of the sole causes a person to lose perspective. You are probably less likely to entrust yourself to others after an injury.

"Rational thought is almost impossible, at least in regard to the hurt and injustice. You might be a person prone to settle the score. You might be tempted toward retaliation to the point that you actually feel as if you committed vengeance. Or, you might be a person who closes inwardly.

"The injured person needs time to rest and sort out thoughts. Any important decisions should be delayed or sorted with trusted council. The injury begins to heal as the injured person can forgive. The forgiveness is begun by confessing to another person. The confession is not a detailed account of the wrong, but to admit, to yourself and somebody else, that you lack the ability to forgive on your own effort.

"The final step of healing is restoration or recovery. Like a bodily injury, the person must ease back into active duty. My leg had to mend itself. The bone had to fuse back together. After the fusion, I had to stretch and work the muscle and tendon connected to the joint to begin to strengthen it.

"Injury of the soul also requires action. The injured person must do something for the person who caused the injury. This is the ultimate act of forgiveness. It also places the injured person back into active duty. The inability to forgive does little or nothing to the person you refuse to forgive. An unforgiving attitude hurts and continues to debilitate the person refusing to forgive.

"Isn't it possible to get accustomed to the pain and almost be afraid you might miss it?" asked Stewart.

"I'm not sure about the psychology of pain, but I know a person can wallow in self pity. You can justify to yourself why you should continue to harbor a grudge. Doing something to demonstrate forgiveness breaks that cycle of self pity as surely as walking and stretching helps a person gain full strength and recovery of an injured limb."

"What do you think you might be doing about your brother?"

"I've been thinking about that. After you have headed for Wellspring, I think I might be heading down to Discovery. I don't know what I might do, but I have to make the effort to contact him."

"I should probably stay here until I'm sure you will be well enough."

"Nonsense boy, you can't hang around here. You need to be getting to Wellspring. That is where you'll find your dreams."

"Since I've met you, I'm not so sure I still have those same dreams."

"You have to go after them. Nobody can give you dreams or take them away. You can only pursue them or forfeit them. I could not let you do that. Sure your dreams change and your realities and perspective change. Your goal is to get to Wellspring. You don't know what the trail will bring between here and the city. You keep pushing in that direction.

"Edward and I knew a miner who was on a claim next to ours. He worked that claim for three years. He put all his resources and energy into finding a vein. He used all his food and about wore out his second pick and shovel. I think he finally just gave out, because he lost hope.

"We noticed we hadn't smelled the smoke from his cook stove for a few days. We decided to climb up around the ridge and over to his camp to see that he was alright. We couldn't find him in his camp, so we went into the shaft. There he was - dead. We decided to bury him there, right in his shaft. As we were digging around to get enough loose aggregate, we saw something shiny. There was the lode of silver. He had been getting so desperate, that he hardly took time to get his lamp and bring it closer to the work. Dim light, no reflection and he could not see the silver ore."

"What about his claim?"

"There was nothing we could do. We all worked so hard, that we didn't take time to visit. There was no address or information about family in his personal effects. Without proper paperwork, in an area that has not been surveyed, you die, you abandon your claim. He had literally reached his dreams, but didn't know it. He'd lost hope because he abandoned the light to guide his path.

"Your dreams are the same way. You might not know exactly what you want, but as you begin to formulate them, you have to stick with it and not give up. When you get closest to your dreams, they will seem furthest from you. Then you will even doubt if they are really your dreams. So, the light that illuminates your journey is the most important constant. You won't recognize your dreams, when you reach them without the light."

"I hope you're right. I just hate to leave you here by yourself. I like to think my motives are only for your welfare, but selfishly, I might be a little anxious of what lies ahead."

Michael responded, "I don't think it is the fear of failure or injury we all face, like those night terrors. I think we fear that our dreams, if reached, won't be as fulfilling as we had imagined."

"I can see that."

"Come on boy! We can talk through another winter. We need to get your victuals ready. You probably have an eight to ten day walk ahead of you."

Michael busied himself, packing hardtack, dried apples, raisins, jerky from the venison Stewart had prepared, sunflower seeds and water. Michael had turned his face so Stewart could not see the tears running down his cheek into his beard.

By Michael's activity, Stewart came to the stark realization: "This was it!" He would be leaving in the morning. The packing put a damper on their usually bright conversations which would have lasted into the night. "We better hit the hay. You'll be leaving early in the morning."

Stewart took a long last look around the cabin. He wanted to cherish this bittersweet moment, this little room and his memories of it forever. He slept without dreams, at least none he could remember. He did not want his last night to go so rapidly. As he awoke, he saw Michael finishing the packing by the light of the lamp. He smelled the coffee brewing on the cook stove and knew he would be eating

Michael's biscuits soon, probably his last real meal until he would reach his destination.

Michael was quieter than usual this morning. Stewart knew why and honored the quiet. Besides, he honestly did not know what to say. Would it seem arrogant to attempt to console another who was saddened by your departure? Was it presumptuous to think Michael was quiet because he was anticipating the departure? Stewart had no answers for his questions.

Shortly, they ate breakfast. Stewart put his possessions together and finished packing as tightly and as concisely as possible. As Stewart finished, he looked up at Michael. Michael was lifting his favorite Winchester from the rack over the fireplace.

"This is yours, boy, you'll need it."

"I can't take that."

"If there is one thing we have taught each other, it is that we accept a gift as a gift. Besides, you would be disrespectful to not honor an old man's wishes."

"I'll only take it if you hang onto my thirty-thirty carbine until I see you again."

"Okay, but where I am going, I won't need the Winchester."

Stewart did not have to ask. He knew what Michael planned to do. As Stewart left, he felt as though in the few months he spent with Michael, he had changed his perspective more than any other time in his life. In fact, he felt as though the past few months had caused everything he had ever learned, thought, or done to suddenly congeal. He felt as though he had been born again.

As he pondered this idea, he could not shake the thought he had been born for adversity. Stewart remembered what Michael taught him. Michael said, "Believe your dreams, trust your instincts, and doubt your fears."

Stewart did not view his present thoughts as fears. He knew well enough what fear was. Rather, he reasoned to himself, they were simply an acceptance of the facts and events before they materialized.

He had only felt this way once before. About a year ago he had a premonition of his gramps dying. The thing he feared most was the loss of his gramps. He had attempted to pass the thought as a childish fear. Then within two months, he was shocked but not surprised when his dad sat him down to tell him the news. God had prepared him beforehand for the tragedy.

Stewart and Michael had talked several times about the descent to Wellspring. They figured, in good weather, the trip would take eight to ten days. If he paced himself and did not attempt too much the first day he would be able to cover more ground each successive day. This thought and the sounds and smell of spring caused Stewart's thinking to return to the farm. In spring, as they began plowing, the horses had to be brought gradually back to the level of work they had achieved per day at harvest.

If the horses were worked too much the first few days, they could be injured or wear-out too soon and then loose more time in recovering. Their best puller, Old Ben, was the slowest to warm-up. In the mornings, especially, in cooler weather, or after he had been worked hard for several days, he was slow to start. He had what Stewart's dad called "cold shoulder." Cold shoulder was a stiffness which was very apparent. Once Ben was stretched and warmed by pulling for a while, he could pull longer days and heavier loads than any of the other horses Stewart's family had ever owned.

Stewart walked about six hours on the first day, watching as the trees and brush became less pervasive and the ridges became rockier. He could see the distinct "edge" called the tree line where the altitude increased so much that not enough air existed for the trees to grow like they did in lower altitudes. He attempted to stay below the tree line if he could. No need to climb over when you could find a way through.

He came to camp early so he could rest and break-in his muscles gradually for the increased strain. He decided he would rest earlier the first day, push himself the second day for about eight to ten hours and get an intermediate day of about six hours again on the third day. He hoped the third day would be about a third of the way.

He also planned to alternate the remaining days between long and short days to rest and recover adequately.

On the afternoon of the third day, Stewart found a small clearing in the trees, boulders and brush. He decided this would be a large enough area to camp. As he began setting up his tent, he had an eerie felling. He looked around to see if there was somebody within sight or sound. There was nobody. As he attempted to rationalize the fear, he became increasingly concerned. Although he heard nothing and could offer no physical evidence for his concerns, he could not shake the feeling.

He decided that if there was another person close by, he should have identified himself. If there was a bear or mountain lion in the area, it was stalking him to decide whether or not to attack. Stewart reached slowly for the Winchester. He controlled his fears because he knew an animal could smell fear and decide to attack for that exact reason. Another man, observing with nefarious motives might take the offensive at the sight of the Winchester.

Stewart quietly and cautiously looked around. He could still see nothing. He decided to break camp and get back onto the trail. While glancing over his shoulder in both directions to look for anything out of the ordinary, he was able to be packed and on his way quicker than usual. As he walked, he kept the Winchester in the ready position, as when he was hunting, instead of over his shoulder on the sling.

The trail above the camp site dipped down behind an abrupt ridge that he could not see beyond until he got to the top of it. As soon as he stepped over the crest of the ridge, he noticed a spot where a doe had given birth to a fawn. The doe and the fawn had gone, but some blood drippings and a placenta remained. Almost simultaneously Stewart stood within a few feet of a mountain lion that had come close to the birthing spot, drawn by the scents.

The lion had not noticed Stewart approaching because he was interested in something else. They both hesitated for an instant. The lion sized Stewart up. Before Stewart had a chance to lift the Winchester, the lion was off into the brush. As he stood there, he realized how alert and intense his concentration had been for the past half hour. He could not remember a time when he had been so focused, as every event seemed to play out in slow motion. He felt confident that the lion made his decision, and was not that interested in him. He walked for about another hour before deciding to camp.

As Stewart set up camp, he kept the Winchester handy. He made sure to secure his pack by throwing a rope over a high limb and hoisting it up away from any predators. Although he had survived an encounter with the mountain lion, he was still more concerned about the potential of having an encounter with a grizzly. He took no shortcuts on precautions.

As Stewart sat by the fire, he reflected back on one of his conversations with Michael. Michael had told him about a Bible character named Jabez. He said the story of Jabez was one of the shortest stories in the Old Testament but carried a huge message. Stewart dug out the Bible Michael had given him. Michael had said, "This is small and handy. Take it with you. I cannot even read it with my glasses any more. I can still read my big book with the large print."

Stewart wondered why men always had to be gruff about things, even when doing something tender hearted. He read I Chronicles four, nine and ten: "Jabez was more honorable than his brothers. His mother named him Jabez, saying, 'I gave birth to him in pain.' Jabez cried out to the God of Israel, 'Oh that you would bless me and enlarge my territory! Let your hand be with me, and keep me from harm so that I will be free from pain.' And God granted his request."

Stewart contemplated all the elements in the simple story that spanned all of two verses. Jabez was honorable. The Bible gave an example of a man asking for a blessing and for his territory to be increased. Finally, Jabez asked for God's hand to be on him to keep him from causing harm and from experiencing pain. God granted his request.

Stewart thought, "Jabez could be me. I can't remember the pain I caused my mother in birth, but I can't shake the felling that I was born for adversity. He kept me from pain and injury this very day, and I hope He will tonight! I have asked for a blessing, although I didn't know I could admit it until Michael taught me this story. I am stepping out to receive God's blessing and an increased territory. I also don't want to cause pain in others."

Stewart remembered how Michael told him about the birds of the air. They did not toil nor worry. They did not go hungry. Even though God provided worms and bugs for the birds, they still had to go out and collect them. Stewart thought back over years of Sunday school, church, family and school, how he had tacitly learned that to seek one's potential was wrong. One should be satisfied with his position in life and not seek self glory. Accepting a station or position in life sounded less like fate and more like 'fatal' to Michael and now to Stewart.

In fact, Michael had insisted that it was selfish, lazy and motivated by complacency to "accept one's station and not improve one's self." Michael argued that God gave us a free will. Sometimes He has protected us and ordered circumstances to get our attention, but He placed the responsibility of choice upon us. In addition God empowered and inspired people to be all that He had created them to be.

Under humble submission to Him, it would be selfish, lazy and complacent not to ask God to bless us, increase our boundaries, and bring healing, not harm to others. Michael had said, "God inspires and empowers us to follow Him. God is not concerned with our ability or inability, only in our availability."

Stewart slept well that night and had vivid dreams. When he awoke, he thought, "Long day. I better get started."

Chapter Twelve

WELLSPRING

As Stewart neared the top of the ridge he could see Wellspring sprawling in the valley below. He was overcome with emotion. His first thought was the joy of nearing the end of the journey. He was then gripped by an irrational fear. The city of his conquest now seemed more threatening than the mountains he had just survived, the mountains of which he was so unfamiliar only eight months ago. He had envisioned this scene in his mind so many times. He had pictured himself conquering the final peak and then triumphantly striding into the city.

Now, however, he sat and stared. He had come so far, now to be overcome with doubt. He had no plan. His glorious ideas seemed to fade. Where would he begin? He wondered if anybody else had felt this way as they reached this peak, so close to their goals. After a short rest, Stewart regained his strength and his courage. He proceeded a little more cautiously than before. He was amazed how much difference some rest, food and water made in his perspective of the situation. He knew the final descent would probably take the remainder of the day.

By dusk, he arrived at the outskirts of Wellspring. In the dusty twilight of the day he passed through "tent town" and neared wood-framed buildings. The distinct center of activity was not as obvious in reality as in his imagination. His picture of the city soon dissolved into streets laden with mud and wagon wheel ruts, dingy buildings - some whitewashed - some covered with weathered lumber - some with wooden bases and canvas roofs. The whole scene was bathed in the smell of wood and coal soot and horse manure.

People were everywhere, going into saloons - carrying supplies, moving, hurrying - all appearing to have a purpose in their efforts. Stewart wondered where he would find Raymond. He then made plans to put-up in the first hotel he saw. Since he had left the farm eight months ago, he had not slept in anything but the make-shift hammock in Michael's cabin and on the ground.

Among the stores, private dwellings and saloons, Stewart saw a marquee, "Travelers' Inn." In the window was a sign, "Room and Bath - $2.00, Meals Extra."

"Good enough," he thought.

After supper, Stewart returned to his room. He missed Michael's company while on the trail, but he had a destination then. Now, he faced the loneliness of the strange room. He previously thought his first night would be a night of celebration. He had, after all, reached Wellspring alive!

The night was dark. The sound of the revelers in the street did not diminish the darkness or the loneliness. His thoughts were more of despondency. He recognized the loneliness and the fatigue. He was unfamiliar with the melancholy. He thought back to the conversations in the cabin when Michael talked about despondency. It was easy to wonder what melancholy actually felt like when you were in good fellowship and in a warm cabin. Maybe he missed the signs of early spring he remembered from the farm, and the family. Maybe he had never attempted goals high enough to experience disappointment. His thoughts centered on a single theme, "Is this all there is?"

In the night, worry was enhanced because nothing could be done about the situation. The next morning Stewart woke with a clearer head. He focused on two tasks. Stewart hoped he could find a job today that would pay at the end of the week. His money would only hold out for food and lodging for a week at most. He also wanted to begin to look for Raymond.

Stewart suddenly remembered the envelope Michael had put in the bottom of his backpack and told him not to open it until he was settled in. Steward thought, "Michael probably wrote me some final words of wisdom, to encourage me and get me started down here."

The warm smile on his face, formed from fond memories, soon turned to a look of awe and amazement. Michael had snuck fifty dollars into the envelope. The note only said, "You will need this more than I will. Be safe, be healthy, and be happy. Remember to guard your perspective and have an attitude of gratitude."

Stewart thought how those words would probably have more impact upon his plans and success than the money, but the money would sure relieve some of the worry about living day to day. "I should probably find a place to check the rifle until I have a place of my own. Maybe I can keep it in the hotel safe until I get situated. I am sure the safe is big enough."

After sleeping past sun up, a bath and breakfast, he checked a board on the front of the inn. The board had different messages tacked on it. Some were personal notes and others were for jobs and help-wanted tags. Some notes appeared to be a few days old, while others, judging from the weathered condition, might be as old as a year. On some tacks, just a corner of paper remained where the rest of the note had weathered or been torn off.

Stewart quickly jotted down some interesting job possibilities with some names and addresses. He also wrote a note for Raymond. He would use the inn as his base of operation until he had a chance to move further into the city.

Stewart began by looking around in the neighborhood in which he was staying. As he looked back up toward the mountains he could see no other distinct trail or road other than the one on which he had entered town, next to the river and the railroad line. He figured Raymond had more than likely used the same trail as he came into town. What type of job did Raymond find?

Stewart thought it best to check some establishments nearby and then proceed to the addresses he had jotted down. He had asked the evening waitress and the night clerk if they had seen Raymond. New people were now filling their shifts so he asked them about Raymond, again to no avail.

By the directions the desk clerk had given him, the first address was about two miles away. In the same fashion that he arrived into town, he had no other form of transportation than walking. The street cars did not yet extend beyond the brick and mortar section of the city. Most of the wood frame structures and wood frame tents were in newly established areas of "town."

As he walked, he noticed a repeating pattern. Every three or four blocks seemed to repeat the previous blocks. There was some type of general purpose store, a saloon, livery stable, hotel, and other types of establishments that might skip several blocks in the general scheme of things, such as land offices, gun shops, chair factories, or wagon wheel factories.

Other blocks might have a hardware store, a market with some fresh vegetables and canned goods; and chickens, turkeys, or bacon hanging under the awning. Less frequently there might be a construction office, or a house that stated, "Boarding by the hour." Stewart wondered why someone would rent a room by the hour. These repeating patterns must have been what he heard called "Neighborhoods."

Stewart did not realize every building he would see for the next several weeks was part of the sprawling growth. The growth was unplanned. If a hotel was successful on one block, someone else thought they might try one in the next new block. Most of the wood framed hotels were actually not much bigger than a four or five bedroom house. Some were called inns, others were called boarding houses.

Most people had not lived on the outskirt long enough to be part of a "Neighborhood." Stewart only noticed one theatre and no libraries. He heard that Wellspring would be the center of knowledge and enlightenment. He was beginning to wonder if the stories were inspired more by romantic impressions of the way people wanted to view the city or if the stories had any validity. After walking about forty-five minutes, he came to Davis Street. He said to himself, "Three-hundred-one, three-hundred-three, yes, three-hundred-nine. There it is, Hagar Townsend Construction."

The office looked make-shift and temporary, as if most of the work done by the company was probably completed on location. The only tasks accomplished in this office were record keeping by Hagar's wife, who also doubled as the receptionist. The office was where people were hired and any negotiating Townsend might do with potential clients.

"Excuse me. Is this Townsend Construction?"

"I think the sign said that." said Mrs. Townsend, glancing up from her work long enough to survey Stewart and then bury her nose in the records again.

"I saw a notice on a bulletin board. Are you still looking for help?"

"We are always looking for help. You just can't find good help anymore. It's not like it was in the good old days when we had some control over the rate of growth. Back then you were part of the city or you didn't belong. It isn't like now. Anybody can get in."

Stewart was not quite sure of what she meant, but he did not care to risk an explanation. What if part of her frustration was the migration of rural people to the city? Or maybe she was upset by the "Orientals" who had stayed after building the railroads. Maybe she did not like former slaves or their families moving out here to find their fortunes or dreams, not to mention their freedom.

Something told him to say only what was necessary to her, and no more. He waited patiently for her to finish what she was doing, as he assumed she was finishing a task which required a lot of concentration. In his youthful, rural naïveté he did not contemplate that she could actually be rude.

While waiting, he casually surveyed the surroundings. He noticed Mrs. Townsend to be about his mother's age and on the heavy side. She wore a shawl. He also noticed the office was dusty with only a desk, a free-standing bookshelf and a rack that contained tubes - probably to organize and protect building plans and drawings. Her desk had several ledgers and stacks of paper and envelopes in no particular order. After a few minutes, she finally said, "As soon as I find an application, you can fill it out."

She found one and handed it to him, "You can read, can't you?"

"Pretty well, I think."

She glanced back at him as if purposely showing no sign of being impressed.

"When could I talk to Mr. Townsend?"

"He will be here at six in the morning before heading out to the job."

"Will I be assured of seeing him if I show up?" Stewart asked as politely as possible.

"Listen, if you want the job, you will be here. We can't give guarantees."

Stewart attempted to conceal his shock. He reasoned with himself, "Maybe city people are just under more pressure."

He didn't know Mrs. Townsend was purposely, through an unspoken arrangement, Mr. Townsend's first line of defense from wasting his time talking to those who were not extremely interested in working. As Stewart left the office and headed back to the hotel, he could not decide whether he felt hope for an early chance at a job or despair over the reception he had received from Mrs. Townsend. He was soon distracted by the bustle of the city.

"Watch out! You country bumpkins ought to look where you are going!" Stewart stepped out in front of a rider who seemed to be galloping fast for the amount of congestion around him.

"Country bumpkin! How did he know I was from the country?" Stewart thought as the rider hurried along, just missing a couple attempting to cross the street. Stewart paid more attention to watching and walking than sightseeing until he reached the inn. He felt a little relieved to be back in the relatively familiar surroundings of the neighborhood. As he reached the front door, he checked the board. His note to Raymond was untouched and he could detect no other new postings. He decided this would be a good time for lunch.

Stewart spent the afternoon making a three block circle, checking every public board he could find in front of the buildings. He decided that if he should get the construction job, he might move closer to the office or to the construction site, depending on how far it was from the office. As he was eating supper, he noticed he missed the first sunset in Wellspring.

Stewart felt more exhausted that night from the uncertainty of not knowing where to find Raymond, and the job situation than from the walking. In fact the walking, on flat ground, lower elevation than the mountains and with no heavy pack seemed to provide enough exercise to refresh him. During the day, he hoped for sleep to escape the reality of his situation. That night he wished he could do more to accomplish his dual tasks.

He awoke with a jolt. He sat erect in bed in the dark for what seemed several minutes before he could catch his bearings. He lit the lamp and glanced at his watch. "Good, four o'clock. I have just enough time to get ready and eat. I hope they are serving early."

When Stewart descended the steps, he could see no signs of life. Maybe he could find something to eat a little closer to the construction office. Having made up his mind, he started into the twilight of the city toward Townsend Construction.

As he found his way through the streets, he could see the sun starting to reflect on the higher peaks of the range west of town. He wanted to stay and watch his first sunrise in Wellspring but found it hard to walk and look back over his shoulder for the sun to appear above the eastern ranges behind him. Stewart knew he must not waste any time if he wanted to eat and arrive at the office ahead of Mr. Townsend. Within a few blocks of Townsend's, by Stewarts estimation, he found a little restaurant with the light on. "Hmm, five o'clock. I'd better get something now."

The smell of bacon and coffee reminded Stewart of his hunger. He thought to himself that he would have found the restaurant without the sign and the light, as the aroma would have led him into the place. Once inside he saw a young waitress of fair complexion. Stewart was intrigued by her mental and physical alertness. She kept the coffee cups filled, took orders and side-stepped off-color comments from rough and crude cowboys, construction workers and other morning men suffering the same fate of having to sweat for a living.

She came and filled Stewart's cup and took his order. Stewart sipped coffee and drank in the smell of food and the atmosphere of the shop. For the first time he began to feel some sort of a warmth to the otherwise cold city. Here, in this little restaurant, he was once again among working men. Although these men were probably not farmers, Stewart found a sense of camaraderie with them.

When she brought his order, Stewart attempted to start a conversation. Although the waitress was busy, she endeavored to be cordial. "I notice you have an accent. Where are you from?"

"I am from Ireland," she replied, brightening with a smile.

She turned and hurried off to fill other cups and bring orders to the other men. Stewart had never heard an Irish accent. He liked it very much. "Oh, well, time to meet Mr. Townsend. I sure hope he is more pleasant than his wife"

Stewart was the first person to arrive in front of the office. He checked his pocket watch. Five forty-five. Now he could relax a few minutes and collect his thoughts, while the sun began to cast long shadows on the buildings around him. "Let's see, I helped with barn raisings. Dad, Gramps and I built the house. I know how to work in a team."

"Good morning. Are you Mr. Townsend?"

"Yes, I am."

"Did Mrs. Townsend tell you I would be here?"

"She mentioned something, but a lot of men have told her they would be here and have not shown."

"I'm looking for work. I have helped…"

"Hold on, let's go inside and sit down for a minute."

As Stewart and Mr. Townsend proceeded into the office, Stewart began to feel a little more at ease. Although Mr. Townsend had a hurried demeanor, he seemed to be more pleasant than his wife.

"So, you have come to the city to find your fortune? The farm could no longer support you and the family, and you have built barns and driven horses?"

"How did you know that?"

"A lot of people are coming to the city from the farms."

"I can work hard and I am willing to give it a try."

"Well, can you start today?"

"Yes, that is why I am here, but I am on foot."

That's fine. You can ride with me today. Tomorrow, if you come back, just meet me at the site. The guys start on the site at six. I usually have to come by the office on my way out."

Stewart was happy to ride in a buggy. He had not been around draft or riding horses since the previous autumn. He was also excited for the opportunity to obtain as much information as he could from Mr. Townsend. At first, he simply enjoyed the city scenes. Even as one not accustomed to city life, he could see this was not yet a city.

It was segments of populations struggling for identity and purpose. He figured the population was growing faster than the city's ability to keep up. Then he remembered that he would have to find the construction site himself tomorrow, so he better pay closer attention to the directions. Maybe over the weekend, he could venture into the original central section of the city.

"Where do most of these people come from?"

"Oh, they come from farms and smaller towns. Some come from cities in the east. Some are from overseas. They hear rumors about wealth and happiness in America."

While they continued to the site, Stewart found Hagar to be quite gregarious. He asked Stewart several questions about his family, his education and farm experiences. Mr. Townsend even asked about Stewart's goals. Stewart had not really thought about specific goals since he left the farm.

"You know, come to think of it, I have dreams, but I never much thought of goals."

"Well, you don't reach your dreams until you set and reach toward your goals. Dreams are like the ridge or mountain you are steering toward. Goals are the steps you take to get there. You can change and alter your goals, but keep your dreams in view."

"Thank you. That sounds like good advice."

Comparing the previous expectations to the present reality almost caught Stewart by surprise. The only goals he had in the last eight months were to help Michael regain his strength and mobility, and to reach Wellspring. Stewart would have given any personal ambitions up in an instant to continue to help Michael. His life had changed drastically and now here he was in the city in which he had imagined himself. Now, on just the second day, the boyish innocence and hope had faded into harsh reality.

"I suppose I want to be in a place that offers more opportunity than I had on the farm."

"Yeah, money is great. Not everyone can get it though. Even fewer of those who do can keep it."

"I suppose so."

"What do you think about being non-union? "

Stewart did not realize his reactions were being scrutinized closely. "I don't mind. I have only heard about the unions. Not much to organize the workers for on a family farm."

"They will destroy us. They are made up of foreign agitators, anarchists and socialists."

As they were talking the thought occurred to Stewart, he was not here for the money. He continued to half-heartedly participate in the conversation as he thought about other things. His participation was not difficult as Mr. Townsend, once engaged, was able to carry the conversation pretty much on his own.

"I think I really want to find more opportunity to learn."

"Oh, you will learn a lot about building, if you can stick with it. I will start you as a hod carrier. Do you know what that is? A hod carrier is a mason's helper. You are not afraid of heights are you? After you learn about bricks and mortar, you will either start laying bricks or help frame. The more skills you learn, the more valuable you are in the trade. "

Stewart realized Mr. Townsend was not hearing him. He asked Stewart questions, but did not always listen to the answers. Stewart could not discipline his own thoughts, let alone convince his new employer of his goals. While Stewart listened he continued to think about Wellspring. He had come for the schools and the resulting professional opportunities. He did not feel like he should tell Mr. Townsend the construction trade was just a conveyance to higher opportunities.

They finally arrived at the site. Stewart was so preoccupied in thought and the appearance of conversation that he could not find his way back if he had to. Mr. Townsend introduced Stewart to the foreman, Big Jim. The building was a three story building of brick and wood frame. Stewart began mixing mortar in a "mud boat" with a tool that looked like an oversized garden hoe with two large holes in it. After mixing he made sure the brick layers kept their boards filled.

As the day wore on and he became increasingly hot and sweaty, he kept one thing in mind. His father always told him, "When you are doing a job, try to keep a positive outlook. Whether you like the work or not, and odds are there will be more you dislike than you like, convince yourself to be happy. You have your health and ability. Learn everything you can in every situation. No experience, no matter how painful or full of drudgery is wasted if you learn and grow from it. Have an attitude of gratitude. If you work with others, try to make them happy. Your day will go faster and you will be well liked."

Stewart was naturally friendly, but he noticed the other men were a little reluctant to accept the "new kid." "I better back off a little. They have been here a while and have seen a lot of kids like me come and go. It will take time to prove myself."

Finally, as the afternoon shadows lengthened into evening Big Jim told the men, "That's it for today."

Everyone seemed to come back to life as they began to clean the mortar off their tools and prepare to head home. Mr. Townsend had a rule that no one was to clean his tools while he was still on the clock. After all, there was plenty of time after a ten hour day to clean their own tools.

The men learned to pace themselves close to lunch or quitting time. They knew how much mortar or "mud" they needed. By gauging their work they could use it up or stretch it out for the last half hour, if necessary. They were not lazy or duplicitous. They did not want to waste a half batch of mortar.

Stewart knew he had to head south to get back to the hotel. He kept an eye on the west ridge as the sun was setting over it. "My first sunset in Wellspring!"

Chapter Thirteen

RAYMOND HAD A PLAN

Back in Discovery, Raymond had a plan! Actually Raymond had two plans, one professional and one personal. The professional plan sounded easy. It was well thought out, logical and sound. Raymond was surprised with himself in the amount of knowledge he had acquired through training at the Mine Institute and from personal experience. The personal goal would take more planning, a whole lot of courage and just plain luck.

Raymond and Mr. Thomas decided on the purchase of a used Ingersoll. It was modified to run on steam that powered an air compressor. The steam engine was similar to some Raymond had seen beginning to appear on the farms down below. Some farmers were actually using those things to pull implements and as a stationary power unit to grind grain, shell corn and even run saw mills.

The advantage of running a compressor to power the drill was that the airlines could reach further into the shafts. The compressor continually blew air into the shaft, which normalized the air and tended to ventilate the shaft by introducing fresh air and blowing out the stale. The normalizing effect was due to the fact that a few feet into the mines, the air stayed a constant fifty-five degrees. Working in an enclosed area or near the opening could get pretty stale and humid. The forced air, as opposed to steam kept dry air moving in the shaft.

Raymond calculated the amount of work the compressor would save. Mr. Thomas wanted to know how much more could be produced by using the compressor. Raymond stalled in answering stating, "We will have to get used to it to see how much we can actually increase production."

The old method with the single and double jack involved a man driving a bit similar in appearance to a large chisel into the rock. As he drove, he rotated the chisel a quarter turn with every hit. This provided neat circular holes in the rock. Double jack drilling involved two veteran miners taking alternate turns in synchronized unity to drive the bit.

They followed the loose quartz when possible as it was most likely to yield the silver and was easier to move than the tightly packed granite. The tunnels had to maintain a certain width and height, in a somewhat straight direction to accommodate the mine carts and rails. So there was a lot of drilling and blasting between the loose veins.

Raymond's plan included getting the men used to the changes in digging due to the mechanization, which would cause fewer people to be involved in the drilling right at the face of the shaft. He wanted to use some of the other men to busy themselves with cutting and placing shoring in the caverns at five or six feet instead of the ten feet Mr. Thomas had been requiring.

Placing shoring at six feet would increase the safety tremendously, but it came with the trade-off of using more man power in the safety aspect than the actual mining. He hoped Mr. Thomas would not inspect the shaft and notice the precautionary improvements. Raymond knew Mr. Thomas wanted the men to be digging and recovering silver, rather than wasting time cutting and placing timbers.

The steam engine, compressor, lines and hammer drill arrived the day before and Raymond was busy supervising the installation. The clerk came to the mine shaft to tell Raymond that Mr. Thomas wanted to see him. As Raymond climbed down the rocky grade, he thought, "Oh no, what have I done now?"

Raymond paused as he entered the office. As he glanced into Victoria's office, he could see that she was watching for him. "Will you be able to make it over for dinner on Sunday?"

"I wouldn't miss it."

As Raymond stood there smiling at Victoria, Mr. Thomas noticed he had entered the office foyer and motioned him to come in. "Raymond, I want you to meet somebody. This is Winston Barlow. I just hired him as a temporary consultant. He has worked in several mines and has some experience with the Ingersoll. This is Raymond Warren, our Foreman. He just came back from a training session on the Ingersoll at the Institute."

""Hi, I am glad to meet you. Where do you come from?"

Raymond had a strange feeling that Mr. Thomas appeared to be chummier with Winston than he was with most employees. He also wondered why Mr. Thomas hired Winston when he had instructed Raymond to make recommendations in his efficiency reports about the optimal number of employees for the work being completed.

"I am glad to meet you too, I came up from Wellspring. I have been around several of the mines, mostly out here in the San Juan's."

"Why don't you show Winston around and then you two can get back to the Ingersoll."

As the two walked, they made small talk. "How did you like the Institute?"

"I thought it was the most intensive two weeks of learning in my entire life."

"Do you think you will be ready for the Ingersoll?"

"Yes, we have Stephen, who has done some mill-righting. He is placing the steam engine and aligning the compressor. We have some other guys building a shack around it to keep the rain and snow off the wood, coal and the machinery."

"Have you had any miners talking about unions?"

"Not really. They feel Mr. Thomas treats them well enough. If they were interested in a union, I don't think they would discuss it with me." Raymond watched Winston's expression as he answered and noticed that Winston was probably doing the same to him. It was an awkward moment, as both men attempted to discern the other's motives in their questions and answers without appearing to be scrutinizing.

They reached the construction project and Raymond introduced Winston to the other men. Raymond watched as Winston got into the action and began assisting in the assembly of the machinery. As Winston worked with different men, he kept a constant conversation going. Raymond thought his questions were sometimes too personal for just having met these men.

The miners carried on just enough conversation so as not to be rude, but kept their thoughts to themselves. They were not too quick to warm-up to strangers and some of them had heard reports from friends and relatives working in other mines to not reveal anything about how you felt about their employer or the working conditions.

They never knew if a stranger might be a union organizer who had infiltrated the ranks, or possibly a Pinkerton spy, working for the owners to ferret out any malcontents and head-off union activity before it started. Whether the stranger was totally innocent or worked for or against union organizing, the men with secure jobs did not want to be caught in the middle. It was better to say nothing rather than to attempt to give an account of what you really meant later, when emotions could outweigh reason.

By Saturday afternoon, the progress on the steam drill project neared completion. Raymond was happy because he would have a good report for Mr. Thomas on Sunday. Raymond had procrastinated on moving from the inn as he was still uncertain whether he needed to be looking for a house or to put-up at the boarding house. After lunch, and a bath, he decided to visit The Mercantile to look over the book selection. He thought a leisurely afternoon, a nap and some reading would be a good way to spend the remainder of the day away from work.

At the Mercantile, he found Victoria looking at books. They spent more time starring into each other's eyes than looking at books. Finally, they each found something to read and Raymond asked, "Would you like to get a cup of coffee?"

"I would love one."

They sat in the inn's dining room for hours until they were finished drinking coffee and just engaged in idle talk. They were totally oblivious of any other people getting a late lunch, eating a dessert or drinking an afternoon cup of coffee. Raymond could not remember a more pleasant afternoon or one in which the time had slipped by so fast. "Would you like to stay for supper?"

"Sure, the roast smells good. I had no idea it was getting so late."

After dinner, Raymond walked Victoria home and said good evening. Upon returning to his room and reading some more, he went to bed, knowing the sooner he went to sleep the sooner it would be Sunday and he would see Victoria. He drifted into and out of conscious thought, unable to distinguish between reverie and actual dreams. The theme was consistent, as the only thing he could focus on was a future with Victoria. He could put up with Mr. Thomas forever if his future included Victoria.

Raymond arrived at his usual time on Sunday. He seemed nervous and edgy and notified Mr. Thomas early in the conversation that he needed to talk to him about something. Victoria gave her usual look of intolerance as she repeated, "No shop talk on Sunday!"

"Oh, this isn't really shop talk. I have a personal matter to discuss with your father. Man talk."

"I suppose!" she exclaimed with a sigh.

After dinner, Mr. Thomas said, "Well, if you two will excuse me."

"Sir, could I have a minute before you go?"

"Sure, walk with me down to the office."

After about a half hour, Raymond returned. Victoria could not decide if he looked more nervous or excited about something. As they finished the dishes together, she asked, "Alright, what was so urgent that you had to discuss with Father?"

"As soon as we finish the dishes, we can talk."

Raymond could not think of a time when he wanted to do something more but was more scared to do it. He kept stalling Victoria about the talk he promised. He finally got the courage and decided to get it over with before he talked himself out of it again. He asked her to sit in the big chair in the living room. He got down on a knee beside her and fumbled for something in his vest pocket. "Victoria, will you marry me?"

Victoria looked surprised. She should have seen this coming, but somehow it still took her by surprise. Raymond felt like time had been suspended in the few seconds it took for Victoria to respond, "Of course!"

Raymond jumped with joy. He could not have looked happier than if he had just discovered the mother lode of silver. "So that's what you had to talk to Father about? What did he say?"

"He said, 'Thank you for asking me. She is a head strong woman, just like her mother. Go ahead and ask her. She makes up her own mind.'"

"So, he didn't mind?"

"Not that I could tell."

"You were gone a half hour. What took so long?"

"Oh, after I talked to your dad, I had to take a walk to rehearse what I was going to say."

"You should not have been so nervous. Couldn't you tell how I felt about you?"

Raymond responded, "Matters of the heart are never certain. Hopes and emotions can cause you to read a lot into a situation."

Raymond calculated his timing, gazed into Victoria's eyes, and gave her a second kiss.

As Raymond made his way back to the inn, he walked past the mining office to see if Mr. Thomas was still there. As he walked past the lighted window, he could see Mr. Conner in the office talking to Mr. Thomas. He decided not to stop.

Inside the office, Mr. Conner asked Mr. Thomas, "So, how is our boy working out?"

"Do you mean Raymond or Winston?"

"Oh, I know how Raymond is working out. Is Winston gaining the confidence of the other workers?"

"I think so. It is early to tell. I think we need to keep the arrangement with him communicating with you, and then you with me."

"Sounds good, I will probably talk to him in a week or two. It will be interesting to see if he thinks he needs to convince them he is an organizer or just another employee."

"Yep. Let's get over to the saloon. Your vest pocket looks like you have some money that needs losing."

Chapter Fourteen

STEWART GROWS WITH THE JOB

Now that Stewart had a job, he decided to find a room closer to the construction site. He also got the brilliant idea that once he had a more permanent address, he could write home and see if they had heard from Raymond. He was reluctant to write and tell his folks that he lost Raymond and was looking for him.

As soon as lunch break started, he went to the boarding house across from the project. He secured a room that provided three meals a day. He decided to get his things after the shift and be back in time for his first supper at the boarding house. He also remembered seeing a post office and a gun shop when he was riding with Mr. Townsend. He could get the letter written tonight and see if the gun shop offered safe storage as a service.

Stewart had a good supper that night. He thought the pork chops were exceptional. The mashed potatoes were almost as good as Mom's. He liked the sauerkraut, although that was not his favorite vegetable. It was difficult to find vegetables in the winter or early spring. Back on the farm, Mom canned enough to feed them into the summer with produce from the vegetable garden. Stewart thought the apple pie and coffee were the best. Ma Peterson, as they called her, claimed she served "working Man's meals." By the way he felt as he climbed the stairs, he could not argue that it was definitely enough to eat.

Upon returning to his room, he hid the Winchester under his mattress. He thought that was probably the first place somebody would look if they broke into his room. "Well, tomorrow after work, I can get it stored safely."

He kept rolling over and over in his mind how he wanted to compose the letter. Fortunately, this letter would be to his mom and dad, and not to Raymond's parents:

Mom and Dad,

I am sorry it took so long to write. I have a long story to tell about how I spent my winter. The short version is that Raymond and I hooked up with another hiker, who was trustworthy enough. I thought it might be some time before I would be able to get back into the mountains, so I took the higher route. Raymond wanted to get through the mountains as quick as possible, so he took the lower route with Daryl.

Before I was very far up the mountain, I found a man who was knocked down by a tree he had chopped. He was pinned under the tree and had a broken leg. I stayed with him and nursed him back to health. He was a fantastic man. You know how I said I wanted to go to school? I feel as though I spent the winter in class with the long discussions we had. His name was Michael Thomas. He gave me a Winchester 45/70 and snuck some money into my backpack when I left.

Unfortunately, I have not been able to reconnect with Raymond. I have posted notices all over Wellspring, close to the trail head where I came out of the mountains. Would you please talk to his parents and see if they have heard from him. I have found a job that should last until next winter.

I am staying at the address I listed, right next to the construction site. Will you try to make it to Wellspring by rail any time this summer? It only takes two days to come around the south end of the San Juan Range by rail. The scenery will not be as majestic as what I saw, but it should be as pleasant ride. Not too costly.

Love,

Stewart

Stewart read the letter over again and placed it into the envelope that he had obtained from Ma Peterson. He wanted to be careful not to alarm anybody without appearing to be too nonchalant in his attitude. Stewart pulled out the Bible Michael sent with him and read until he was ready to fall asleep. It did not take long with the full day's work, the walk and the heavy supper before he got up, put out the lamp and climbed back into bed.

Stewart slept in a little longer than usual since he did not have to find a place to eat breakfast or walk to the job site. Stewart was on the site mixing mortar and stacking bricks when the other men started filtering in. He always brightened when he saw Sven. Sven was a large framed Swedish man with a heavy accent. Sven was a fatherly figure with a huge heart.

Stewart asked Sven how many blocks up the street the post office might be and if the gun shop stored guns as a service. Sven got a big grin on his face and said, in his Swedish accent, "Iis Stewart writin' hist girlfriend?"

Stewart laughed and said, "No, I am finally writing home, now that I have an address where they can write back."

Sven told Stewart that the post office and gun shop were about five to seven blocks west and about two blocks apart. Stewart figured he would not be able to get everything done during his lunch and be back in time. He would go after work. Maybe Big

Jim would let him knock off about a half hour early, if he got everybody supplied with bricks and mortar.

Stewart asked the favor. Big Jim said, "I guess, but don't make it a habit."

Stewart worked ahead of the bricklayers so he had more than enough bricks for them to finish the afternoon. He made an extra batch of mortar and covered it in the mud boat so it would not dry too quickly. He asked Sven if he would clean the boat, the mortar boards and the square nose shovel. Sven laughed and said, "You can't efen finish der verkday vit' out running off to see dat girl?"

Stewart just laughed and headed for the boarding house. He wanted to get everything worked out and be back for supper. He reached under the mattress and pulled out the Winchester, grabbed the envelope and headed out. He got some weird looks as he walked down the street carrying a Winchester rifle, but he had encountered that the other times he had to move the gun in town. He arrived at the post office, bought a stamp and asked how long the letter would take by rail. The clerk said, "Oh, about a week."

Stewart walked another block and a half and found the gun shop. While he was waiting for the store owner to finish with another customer, he looked around at the guns and ammo. The smell of gun oil, the leather holsters and the shining precisely machined parts on the guns made Stewart think of Gramps.

Although Gramps was not a gunsmith, people brought their guns to him to fix from miles around. In fact they brought everything they could not figure out themselves. Gramps had taught himself the machine shop, welding, forging, and blacksmithing. Gramps could even pick the guitar in the evenings. Stewart wondered what Gramps could have accomplished if he were born a couple of generations later, in the Industrial Revolution. Well, I guess we are all created for our time. What do we do with it?

"Do you want to sell that?"

"What? Stewart realized the shop owner was talking to him. No sir, but do you offer secure storage of guns for customers?"

"But you're not a customer."

"If I buy some ammo and pay for the storage, I am a customer."

"I guess that is true. Two bucks a month."

"Done. How often do you want me to check in to pay? "

"Pay the first two months and then check in and pay each month."

Stewart got a receipt and left, promising to buy ammo when he needed it. As Stewart walked back to the boarding house, he felt relieved to have made the effort to communicate with home and he felt the gun was secure. He also looked for any messages on the sign boards he passed.

As he passed a café, he could see Mr. Townsend talking to three men. Mr. Townsend was facing away from the window so he could not see Stewart. Stewart took a quick glance at the other men and continued toward supper. He thought as he walked. He wondered who those men were, and why Mr. Townsend was talking to them away from the office. One had a suit on and looked more like an attorney than a construction worker.

Stewart wondered if Mr. Townsend was hiring any more workers. From the quick glance, Stewart discerned that the conversation was one between men familiar with each other and not the tense or formal type of conversation in which somebody was seeking employment from the other.

The next day at work Sven said, "Stewart, vee talk sometime today, yah?"

"Sure, we talk all the time during the day."

"No, I mean in private."

"Okay, let's get something to drink after work and talk. It's Friday, and I feel like celebrating a little"

At the end of the shift, the men cleaned their tools, picked up their gloves, coats and lunch boxes. Stewart wondered all afternoon why Sven was so secretive. They walked down the block to the saloon, found a semi private booth and ordered something to drink. "Alright, Sven, what do you want to talk about?"

"Stewart, has anybody approached about der union?"

"Nobody has. I guess I would be willing to listen."

"You don't vant to talk about der union on der job. Townsend vould fire you at der drop of der hat if efen he thought you ver interested in listnin'. If he thought you ver an infiltrator, or an agitator, he vould haf you beaten and driven off."

"Oh, that's crazy. That would be against the law, and what is he so afraid of?"

"Oh, don't get me wrong. I'm no union organizer. I just vant you to be avare of vat ist happening. Der owners und people who haf der vealth are not villing to share der fortune wit dos upon whose shoulders dey built dare vealth. Dey say der unions are Socialistic. Der unions say dey vant safe verking conditions und fair wages. It's not about vat ist right and wrong. It's about total control."

"But, what about those thugs who are being hired to suppress peoples' right to free choice?"

"Dey are private detectives hired by der Pinkerton Agency. Dey are all over der Vest in mining towns, construction sites and on der railroads. Some infiltrate, posing as union organizers. If dey sense dat an employee ist sympathetic toward der union, dey might play along and set der person up. Dey haf efen been alleged to organize strikes to shut der union down. Dey act as judge, jury and executioner. None haf been prosecuted, as day haf efen been used by governors and local law enforcement agencies. Dey are abuff der law. Dey consider themselves to be der law. Be careful Stewart, I could efen be von."

"On that, I remain dubious."

"Chust be careful, yah!"

By Sven's expression, Stewart knew he was not kidding around. Sven always tried to make the job easier for the other workers. He attempted to bring humor into every aspect of the job. He was a father figure to younger men, and teased them about girl friends, work habits and appetites. Although he teased Stewart, Stewart never felt like the teasing was a put-down or mean spirited. Although Sven was one of the older men on the job, he was like working with a great big kid. Stewart thought, "Dad would like Sven and he would be happy to know someone was keeping an eye on me."

On Monday Big Jim approached Stewart. He looked concerned as he pulled Stewart aside to talk to him. "What did you and Sven talk about Friday after work?"

Stewart attempted to show no emotions as he answered. "Nothing. We just stopped and had a drink after work."

"Just be careful who you listen to. You know there are troublemakers everywhere."

Stewart was now seething under the surface that his foreman would actually keep track of who visited who after work. "Sven has been nothing but kind to me. He even warned me about unions."

"You might reconsider mentioning that word on this site."

"Yes sir!"

As Big Jim finished talking and began to turn around, Stewart noticed some of the other men watching and trying to eavesdrop on the conversation. He could not describe it, but Big Jim's attitude seemed to abruptly change toward him. Previously, Big Jim had at least feigned an air of friendliness. As Stewart worked the rest of the day, the other men also seemed to distance themselves from Stewart and Sven, almost as if they no longer trusted them. Stewart was amazed how the men had judged and convicted him and Sven without a chance at any defense. Gramps was right when he told Stewart, "Facts are negotiable, perceptions are not."

Stewart had only been able to trust Big Jim on a limited basis, even prior to this conversation. In other conversations, Big Jim would act respectful to somebody's face, only to make a comment about the person to Stewart after the person left the immediate area. He even acted respectful toward Mr. Townsend, only to make sly comments about him in his absence.

Stewart even suspected that Big Jim, in an effort to maintain control and dependency from the workers, had spread bad reports

about the men to Mr. Townsend. Big Jim was more likely to reward
the workers for demonstrating outward respect for him than the
amount of work they were able to produce. Big Jim liked to think
the workers respected him. They actually feared his devious tactics.
When he wasn't around, they referred to him as "Jumbo."

Toward the end of the day on Thursday, the men began cleaning
their tools. Big Jim called Sven over to talk to him, before Sven had
finished. The men left after they cleaned their tools. Stewart hung
around until Big Jim left the site. "Would you like some help?"

"You run along, boy. I am almost done. You don't vant to keep
dat girl vaitin.'"

Stewart went directly to his room, poured some water in the basin
and began to wash his face and hands. As he was drying his hands,
standing back away from the window, he could see Sven arguing
with two men. They were inside the building, almost obscure from
sight. They would not have been seen from the ground, but were
visible from Stewart's vantage point. The encroaching darkness
almost hid them in the shadows.

As one man talked face to face to Sven, the other had sidled around
behind him. Stewart looked more closely as that man picked up a
wooden plank and swung it, hitting Sven on the head and knocking
him to his knees. The two men ran so quickly that Stewart did not
have time to do anything but watch. He clearly saw their faces as

they neared the street. He saw them as they stopped running and began walking rapidly down the street.

Stewart ran down the steps. Ma Peterson had dozed in her chair since Stewart came in from work and greeted her. He shouted to wake her and to tell her to find help and send somebody to the police. Stewart ran over to assist Sven. He found Sven alive, but

unconscious, bleeding pretty badly from the head wound. As Stewart attempted to comfort Sven and support his head, a police officer came upon the scene. Stewart thought that was awfully quick, but he was thankful he arrived so quickly.

"Alright, put him down and step away."

"Officer, I didn't do this."

"I am sure you didn't."

About this time some men from the boarding house came and made a make-shift stretcher. They carried Sven to a bed on the ground floor in the boarding house. Another man had gone to retrieve the doctor. As the men were taking care of Sven, the police officer placed Stewart in hand cuffs and led him away. "I can explain!"

"I am sure you can. Save it for the judge."

Stewart knew he should not attempt to tell anybody what happened until he had an attorney or someone he felt he could trust. The officer took Stewart to the nearest jail, got him checked in and told the men he was off duty now, and he would see them tomorrow. Stewart later learned the officer's name was, Kevin Nelson.

The jail was a small building with four small cells - about eight feet by six feet iron cages. Stewart was beside himself. He was worried about Sven and he knew this whole situation could go very badly for him. After about two hours, Ma Peterson came to the jail. She told Stewart the doctor had examined Sven and tonight would be very difficult, but if he survived until morning, he would probably live. She also told Stewart that she had a nephew who was an attorney. She had sent word to him to meet with Stewart in the morning, as he would have to stay overnight. She also brought him his Bible and the jailer approved of letting him have it to read.

Stewart was reading Proverbs: "Anyone who rebukes a mocker will get insults in return. Anyone who corrects the wicked will get hurt. So don't bother correcting mockers; they will only hate you. But correct the wise and they will love you."

Stewart was thinking how he had never really met anybody he would consider wicked. He also wondered how mockers behaved. About midnight Stewart heard a commotion in the outer office of the jail. Two other police officers brought in two men, who were charged with being drunk and disorderly at a saloon. Stewart was still reading. As he looked up, he recognized the men. He did not know if they had ever seen him or would recognize him. He tried to keep his face turned away from them as much as possible as they were placed in two of the other cells on the other side of the room.

"Hey Julius, look we have a Bible scholar. They only read that thing when they get themselves into trouble."

Without looking up or turning his face toward the men, Stewart asked, "Don't you believe in the Bible?"

"It's for suckers. It's a bunch of fables used to make people feel guilty and to control us."

Stewart did not want to engage in too much conversation, but he could not resist asking a few questions. He wanted to see if he could discover anything about the motives of these two men. "Actually I read it every day."

"If you're so good, why're you in here?"

"I didn't say I was good. But I can be forgiven. How about you?" Stewart asked the other man, "Do you believe this is just fables or do you believe in God?"

"What difference does it make? There's no hope for any of us."

Stewart said, "There is hope, but we have to believe."

"Oh great! We got locked-up with a preacher."

The officer opened the door, shut off the light and said, "Alright you guys, shut-up and get to sleep."

Stewart spent the night praying for Sven to recover.

The next morning, Ma Peterson came with her nephew, James Peterson.

He informed Stewart that it looked like Sven was going to make it, although he was still unconscious. They were going to wait until Saturday morning to see if he would be stable enough to be moved to the hospital. "We have some other good news. Since there was no murder, and they can only charge you with attempted murder or assault and battery, a bail hearing is set for nine A.M."

The jailer came in and handcuffed Stewart. They escorted him to the barred police wagon to take him to the court house. James said, "I will drop Aunt Irene at home and meet you at the court house."

Stewart made bail and was given the date of the hearing. Bail was set at two hundred and fifty dollars, so he paid twenty-five. He asked James when they could talk, and they set aside a time for Saturday morning. Stewart went to work, but was told that until he got cleared, they would not allow him on the job site. Fighting with another employee was strictly forbidden by Townsend.

Stewart looked in on Sven. He wondered how anybody could provoke such a decent person and injure or attempt to kill him. As Stewart was thinking about the turn of events he decided to do some detective work of his own. He knew he had seen Sven's attackers, prior to the evening of the attack. He was trying to think why they looked familiar to him when he saw them fleeing the scene. As he walked past the café where he had seen Mr. Townsend, he realized they were the two men talking to Mr. Townsend. "Who was the fourth man?"

Stewart went to the saloon where the men had been arrested. It was only a half block from the construction site. They apparently did not feel the need to run very far. They probably got drunk to drown their guilt, if they had any conscience. Stewart asked the bartender if he knew the men. He knew their names, but not much else. Stewart took the names, August and Julius Knapp.

Chapter Fifteen

THE TRIALS OF LIFE

On Saturday, Stewart showed up at the law office for his first meeting in preparation for his trial. He told James about the policeman who arrived on the scene within minutes, assuming that Stewart was guilty. He also relayed that the two men he saw fleeing were in jail later that night and they had been arrested only a half block from the construction site.

James asked Stewart if he thought the men might have recognized him. He said they could not have seen him unless they had previously been casing the construction site and had seen him there. James took their names and said he would do some checking of his own.

Stewart asked James how close the library might be. James said it was quite a distance into the Central City, but Stewart could walk part way and catch a trolley. Stewart went to the library and checked through the newspaper archives from the past two months.

He looked for any information about arrests for assault and battery, union busting and Pinkerton Detective Agency work.

In an article from six weeks earlier, Julius and August had been arrested in a "workplace disturbance." Charges were dropped due to "insufficient, conflicting and circumstantial evidence." There were allegations that the two worked for the Pinkertons, but that evidence was not allowed into the proceedings. As Stewart studied the article, he looked at the photograph of the prosecutor, Mr. Connor. That was the man in the suit, talking to Mr. Townsend and the Knapp brothers in the café.

When Stewart got back home, he asked Ma Peterson how Sven was doing. "The swelling has gone down. The doctor thinks he can be moved to the hospital. He is a very lucky man."

Stewart was not very hungry, but managed to eat a little. After supper, he went up to his room and thought about the week earlier, when he and Sven had talked after work. As he thought, he glanced over to the construction site. Things seemed so simple then. There were no worries except to keep sharp on the job and stay ahead of the brick layers. "It looks like they are making progress, even without Sven and me on the job."

Stewart read the verses he was reading the previous night in jail. He was amazed how much relevance the verses had to his situation. He also read in Psalms, "Do not take my soul away along with sinners, nor my life with men of bloodshed. And whose right hand is full of bribes. The Lord is my light and my salvation; whom shall I fear? The Lord is the defense of my life, whom shall I dread? When evildoers came upon me to devour my flesh, my adversaries and my enemies, they stumbled and fell."

How much more real those verses seemed after obtaining new evidence. Stewart hoped the promise at the end would hold true. "…they stumbled and fell…"

The hearing was a week and a half later. James and Stewart were seated at the defense table when Mr. Connor found his place at the prosecution table and began laying out documents and evidence.

Stewart saw him smile at the Knapp brothers as they seated themselves. He also glanced at Mr. Townsend sitting in the back of the court room and gave a slight nod in his direction. The bailiff said, "All rise for the honorable Judge Baldini."

James slid Stewart a writing tablet and said, "Anything you want to say to me, write it here and slide it over."

Judge Baldini said, "This is a pre-trial hearing to determine if Stewart Taylor should be tried for the attempted murder and assault and battery of Sven Erickson, a co-worker at Townsend Construction. It will be a little less formal than a jury trial, although we will follow the same procedures. I will weigh the evidence and decide whether to proceed. Prosecution, opening statement, please."

"Your honor and observers, the State intends to prove that Mr. Taylor did intentionally and deliberately assault Mr. Sven Erickson on the evening of March twentieth, nineteen hundred and six, at about ten minutes after six. We have witnesses who saw Mr. Taylor attack Mr. Erickson. The police officer who was first on the scene completed the investigation."

Judge Baldini said, "Defense, opening statement."

"Your honor, the defense intends to prove that Mr. Taylor did not have time or motive to commit this beating of Mr. Erickson. The prosecution is basing their case on circumstantial evidence, sloppy detective work and nefarious motives of their own to divert the attention of the legal system regarding the actions of the groups with which the alleged witnesses associate. We can demonstrate that Mr. Taylor is innocent of the charges."

Judge Baldini, "Prosecution may call their first witness. "

"The prosecution calls Julius Knapp."

Bailiff, "Place your right hand on the Bible. Do you solemnly swear to tell the truth, the whole truth and nothing but the truth, so help you God? "

"I do."

"Do you recognize this man? Let the record show, I am pointing at Stewart Taylor?"

"Yes."

"Where have you seen him?"

"I saw him hit Mr. Erickson with a plank of wood."

"Thank you, no further questions"

Judge Baldini said, "Defense cross?"

"Where were you when you saw Mr. Taylor hit Mr. Erickson?"

"I was on the sidewalk in front of the construction site."

"Was the construction site dark or lit?"

"It was just starting to get dark."

"How could you tell the weapon was a plank?"

"I just figured it was. A shovel would have been handy and all."

"So, you are guessing it was a plank of wood?"

Julius's eyes widened as he instinctively looked over at Mr. Connor, who quickly nodded his head to the affirmative. "Yes, I guess it was a plank of wood."

"Did you stop to see if Mr. Erickson was injured?"

"No officer Nelson arrived on the scene almost immediately. We figured he had the situation under control."

Mr. Peterson asked, "Did officer Nelson arrest you?"

"No."

"How did you know the officer was Officer Nelson?"

Mr. Connor, "I object!"

Judge Baldini answered, "Overruled. Answer the question."

Julius once again looked at Mr. Conner with wide eyes and a panicked expression.

Judge Baldini said, "The witness is advised to answer the question."

Julius fumbled, "He, uhm ... uhm, Officer ... uh, Nelson questioned me that night."

Mr. Peterson asked, "Point of order, your Honor. These proceedings carry the same weight for perjury as a regular trial, is that correct?"

Judge Baldini answered, "That is correct."

"Thank you, your Honor." Turning back toward the witness, "You did not volunteer to Officer Nelson that you had witnessed the attack?"

"No."

"Were you arrested later that night?"

"That was a misunderstanding."

Judge Baldini, "Answer yes or no, please."

"Yes we were."

"Did you make fun of the other prisoner for reading the Bible?"

"No."

"Did you say, 'There's no hope?'"

"How'd you know that?"

"I will ask the questions. I am finished with him, your honor."

Mr. Connor questioned August Knapp and established the same story.

Judge Baldini asked, "Defense cross?"

"Mr. Knapp, please describe what you saw on the evening in question."

"I saw Mr. Taylor hit Mr. Erickson with some type of pole or long handle."

"Other than the night that you allegedly saw Mr. Taylor strike Mr. Erickson, do you ever remember seeing Mr. Taylor?"

"No, just today in court."

"Do you mean to tell me that you saw Mr. Taylor strike Mr. Erickson and you could remember him from almost two weeks ago, but you did not recognize him in jail that night?"

"The construction site was getting dark! "

"So you could not really see him well enough that night to recognize him six hours later?"

"We were drunk later."

"Did you make fun of Mr. Taylor for reading the Bible?"

"That was him?"

"I will ask the questions."

"Did you say, 'People only read the Bible when they are in trouble?'"

"Maybe something like that."

"Do you believe in God?"

"What difference does that make?"

Mr. Connor shouted, "Objection!"

Judge Baldini asked, "Council?

James said, "I can establish relevance, your Honor."

"Proceed, but let's get there quickly."

"Do you know where the laws of the land originate, such as do not steal, do not commit murder, and do not bear false witness?"

"The Ten Commandments, I suppose."

"If you don't believe in God, what difference does it make whether you kill a man?"

"You could get caught."

"So it only matters to you whether you get caught or not?"

"You are twisting my words. "

Judge Baldini reminded him, "Answer with yes or no, please."

"Do you believe in God?"

"People only turn to Him when they are desperate."

"Then how can we believe any of your testimony when you swore to tell the truth on the Bible?"

"They told me to swear on the Bible."

"What if they told you to bear false witness or to beat somebody yourself? "

Mr. Connor said, "Objection, the witnesses are not on trial here."

Under his breath, James said, "They should be."

Judge Baldini said, "The defense is reminded to keep their comments to themselves."

"I am sorry, your honor. No further questions."

Judge Baldini directed, "Prosecution, next witness."

Mr. Conner stated, "The prosecution calls James Swanson."

Big Jim was sworn in.

"Mr. Swanson, how are you involved in this situation?"

"I am the foreman on the construction site for Mr. Townsend."

"Do you believe Mr. Taylor had motive to hit Mr. Erickson?"

"Objection, that calls for speculation."

"Sustained."

"Let me rephrase. Did anything peculiar happen at work that week?"

"Yes, I know Mr. Erickson and Mr. Taylor had words after work one evening before the fight."

"Thank you. That is all."

Judge Baldini asked for the defense to cross examine.

James asked, "Do you mean the two men argued after work?"

"Not really."

"How did you know they talked away from work?"

"Some of the men told me."

"So, you cannot say they had heated words, or even have firsthand knowledge of their conversation?"

"I guess not."

"Did you warn Stewart to be careful to whom he talked?"

"Yes."

"Why?"

"He was a good worker. I didn't want him to get into any trouble."

"Was his discussion outside of work really any of your business?"

"No."

"The defense is finished with this witness."

"Does the prosecution have any more witnesses?"

"No, your Honor."

"The defense may call their first witness."

"The defense calls Mrs. Irene Peterson."

Ma Peterson was sworn in.

"Mrs. Peterson, how do you know the defendant?"

"I run the boarding house right across from the construction site. Mr. Taylor rooms there. He is a wonderful boy. "

Judge Baldini instructed, "Just answer the questions please, Mrs. Peterson"

"Did Mr. Taylor come home after work on the day in question?"

"Yes, he did."

"How long was he home?"

"I would say about fifteen or twenty minutes."

"Did you see the Knapp brothers when you watched Stewart run to the construction site?

"No."

"Thank you. The defense rests."

"Would the prosecution like to cross examine the witness?"

"Mrs. Peterson, are you the aunt of Mr. Peterson, the council for the defense?"

Mr. Peterson exclaimed, "Objection! Relevance?"

"Sustained."

"How do you know how long Mr. Taylor was home?"

"I saw him come in. I looked at the clock and it was about five after six. I heard him up in his room getting ready for supper, like he usually does. He washes his face and hands."

"What was the next thing you heard?"

"Stewart came running down the steps, shouting for help. I woke up and watched where he went. He ran over to the construction site. A minute later, I saw Officer Nelson arresting him. It was so quick; there was no time for a fight. It had to have already happened."

"How do you know the fight had not already happened and he came home for an alibi?"

"His shirt was clean when he came in, except for dirt from the construction site. He later got his shirt bloody attempting to help Mr. Erickson."

Stewart was called to testify. He recounted how he saw the incident from his room. That was when he ran out. He identified the Knapp bothers as the attackers. Finally, Mr. Peterson asked, "Had you seen these men before?"

Stewart said, "I saw them, Mr. Townsend and Mr. Connor talking at a café about a week before the attack."

Mr. Peterson handed a copy of the arrest report to Stewart. "Have you ever seen this?"

"No."

"It was not filled out that evening with Officer Nelson?"

"No, he turned me over to the jailer and said, 'That is the end of my shift. I will see you tomorrow.'"

"Your honor, it is too bad Officer Nelson is not here to verify the validity of this arrest report. By the date, it appears to have been completed the next morning, as the Knapp brothers were added as witnesses."

"Objection, your Honor. Is the defense testifying?"

"Overruled, you may proceed."

"Your honor, the defense moves to strike this report as invalid, since the officer was not called to validate it, and they did not even find the witnesses or talk to them that night, prior to their own arrests."

"I will take that under advisement."

At that moment, there was a commotion at the back of the court room. Sven was awake and being wheeled into the courtroom in a wheel chair. Judge Baldini exclaimed, "Order in the court or I will have this room cleared!"

"Your Honor, the defense would like to call Mr. Erickson to the stand."

"Objection, the people have not been advised of this witness."

"Overruled, Mr. Erickson may be sworn in."

Sven was sworn in. "Mr. Erickson, did Mr. Taylor attack you or, to the best of your knowledge, have any reason to assault you?"

"No, it vas dose two," Sven replied, pointing at the Knapp brothers. "One vas talking to me from der front, vile de udder snuck around und hit me from behind. I turned chust in time to see him swingin' der vooden plank. See, der gash ist right here across der side of my head."

Mr. Peterson came to his feet, "Your honor, I move the charges against my client be dropped. I also request that a special prosecutor be called to investigate the connection between Mr. Connor and the Knapp brothers."

Judge Baldini exclaimed, "The Court finds insufficient evidence to proceed to trial! The matter of calling a special prosecutor is beyond my jurisdiction. Case dismissed!"

All the observers in the court room cheered, except the Knapp brothers, Mr. Conner and Big Jim. Mr. Conner had some heated words for the Knapp brothers; although he was not loud enough for others to hear what was said. Townsend had already walked out. He looked at Big Jim and they shrugged their shoulders offering a disgusted look as if they were the victims.

James extended his hand to Mr. Conner, who did not extend his. James said, "This isn't over."

Conner retorted, "You're just a fart in a skillet, some Johnny-come-lately, out to make a name for himself."

"We'll see."

Stewart could not hug Sven because of the wheel chair and bandages. They shook each other's hands and grasped their left hands across the top of their right hands. Stewart said, "I prayed a lot for you."

Sven replied, "I know you did boy. Der doctor said it vas a miracle, especially dat first night dat I lived. He says I am doing fine. Chust need rest."

"Will you go back to Townsend's?"

"I don't tink dey vant me. I vould not go back anyway. Dare are a lot of construction jobs in dis town."

Stewart suggested, "Let's keep in touch. You know where I am."

"I vill, boy! I vill."

That night Stewart read: "I prayed to the Lord and He answered me. He freed me from all my fears. Those who look to Him for help will be radiant with joy, no shadow on their faces. In my desperation I prayed, and He listened; He saved me from all my troubles. For the angel of the Lord is a guard; He surrounds and defends all who fear Him."

Stewart prayed, "Thank you, Lord for protecting and defending me. You satisfy all my needs and take away all my fears. I have one more concern. I will not call it a fear, but I will probably need a job."

Stewart decided to go to church on Sunday. He regretted that he had not been looking for a church since he left home. Then he remembered the verse, "Where two or more are gathered in My name, I am among them." Stewart thought, "Michael and I were in church several times a week, not just on Sunday."

Stewart asked Ma Peterson where they went to church. She told him the times of services and gave him directions on how to get there. He asked, "What denomination is the church?"

Ma Peterson chuckled a little. "I have not heard anybody ask about the denomination for some time now. It is non-denominational."

He thought out loud, "Well, it's worth looking into."

As Stewart entered the church building, he observed the people going in to worship. Everybody seemed happy and friendly. Several people greeted him warmly. He noticed that not everybody looked the same as him. There was a Chinese family in the pew in front of him. There were several families that were either former slaves or descendents of slave families. He also heard some Scandinavian accents and a different family that appeared to be Hispanic, consisting of several generations.

He enjoyed the music as the opening hymns were *Amazing Grace* and *It is Well with My Soul* - his absolute favorite hymns in the world. The emotion of worshipping in a church building with an organ player, combined with the long absence from formal church; the friendliness of the congregation members; the joy of Sven's recovery; and, the charges being dropped made it impossible for Stewart to conceal his tears of joy.

The preacher stood up and smiled, as he motioned the congregation to take their seats. "Today, I want to conclude my sermon on *Radical Christianity*." Do you remember what the word 'radical' means? Radix is the word for 'root.' Radical means going back to the original meaning of what we learn and do. Radical also means reform that goes back to the roots. It is chopping out a bad tree by the roots, rather than constantly raking the leaves. To eradicate is to take something out by the roots. We are not Protestant. We are pre-Protestant Christians!

"I want to keep politics out of the church, but when you discuss something with somebody and they do not agree, they may resort to labeling you rather than discussing the issues. Even in this great land of ours, people will still attempt to dominate your thoughts, try to convince you to think like them and even control or suppress you if you think differently.

"If you disagree politically, they will label you progressives, muckrakers, reformers, radical, and the dreaded - socialist. They will hide behind Democrat, Republican, Liberal, and Conservative. What is the answer in these trying times? Go back nineteen hundred years. What did Jesus say? Was Jesus Catholic, Mormon, Methodist, capitalist, or socialist? There are some truths, although partial truths in all of these philosophies and religions.

"I won't attempt to tell you the difference between philosophy and religion - they are too similar. Jesus said, 'Your treasure is where your hearts is.' James said, 'Out of the abundance of your heart, your tongue speaks.' That which you worship will be your god. That which you think is serving you, is your master.

"I can tell you the difference between religion and faith. Religion is making God into our desired image of Him through rules, regulations and traditions of men, and 'good' living.

Religion keeps more people from God than any other man-made institution. Faith is reaching out to God as a sinner and asking for forgiveness. It is asking Him to dwell in your heart and, through the Holy Spirit, inspiring and empowering you to live beyond your abilities and limitations."

"Amen! Preach it, Brother!"

"Did Jesus talk about politics? Did He talk about social reform? Did He address the worker and employer relationship? You tell me. I will share a few passages. On being radical, He said your life should reflect your faith. James, one twenty-two through twenty five says, 'Do not merely listen to the word, and so deceive yourselves.' Do what it says. 'Anyone who listens to the word but does not do it is like a man who looks at his face in the mirror and, after looking at himself, goes away and immediately forgets what he looks like. But the man who looks intently into the perfect law that gives freedom, and continues to do this, not forgetting what he has heard, but doing it - he will be blessed in what he does.'

"So, 'Do the Word!' What are some other examples? Proverbs thirty-one eight and nine says, 'Speak up for those who cannot speak for themselves, for the right of all who are destitute. Speak up and judge fairly; defend the rights of the poor and needy.'

"Do not love money. Paul tells us in First Timothy, chapter six, verse ten, 'The love of money is the root of all evil.'

"About the employee-employer relationship, James says:

> Now listen, you rich people, weep and wail because of the
> misery that is coming upon you. Your wealth has rotted, and
> moths have eaten your clothes. Your gold and silver will testify
> against you and eat your flesh like fire. You have hoarded wealth
> in the last days. Look! The wages you failed to pay the work-
> men who mowed your fields are crying out against you. The
> cries of the harvesters have reached the ears of the Lord almighty.
> You have lived on earth in luxury and self-indulgence. You have
> fattened yourselves in the day of slaughter. You have condemned
> and murdered innocent men, who were not opposing you.

"Bosses and company owners, learn what James had to say
about how to treat your employees. There will be no need for
people to organize. Bad management makes good unions. There
will be no need to control peoples' free choice. They will follow
you gladly.

"Workers, Colossians says, 'Whatever you do, work at it with
all your heart, as working for the Lord, not for men.' Work to
receive your reward from God. Work the same when your boss is
watching as when he isn't because God sees all.

"Was Jesus a tax reformer? In His time, tax gatherers were
some of the most corrupt people around. They were used as an
example with prostitutes, drunkards, gluttons, and other people
of questionable character. On two occasions people tried to test

Him to see if He was a tax evader, or if He would call down the supernatural to reform the system. On one occasion, He simply asked, 'whose picture is on the coin?'

"They said, 'Caesar.'

"He replied, 'Give unto Caesar that which belongs to Caesar. Give unto God that which belongs to Him.' God wants the hearts of men and women.

"The other time, a disciple asked Him if they should pay taxes. Jesus told him to go catch a fish, look in his mouth and retrieve the coin. 'Then pay taxes for you and Me.'

"In closing, don't try to change people. Don't label them if they think differently than you. Change your mind. Be radical. Seek to understand before you attempt to make somebody understand you.

"He wants you to renew your mind. Paul, in Romans twelve, one and two, said, 'Therefore, I urge you, brothers, in view of God's mercy, to offer your bodies as living sacrifices, holy and pleasing to God — this is your spiritual act of worship. Do not conform any longer to the patterns of this world, but be transformed by the renewing of your mind. Then you will be able to test and prove what God's will is — His good, pleasing and perfect will.'"

On his walk home, Stewart thought, "These are the things Michael and I discussed so often. How can I live them?"

When he returned to the boarding house, James Peterson was there for Sunday dinner. He told Stewart that he had drafted a letter to the governor requesting a special prosecutor in the connection of Mr. Connor, the Knapp brothers and the Pinkerton agency.

Stewart asked, "Do you think it will get anywhere?"

"Not unless we try. These people are so brazen about their feelings of entitlement that whether we can stop them or not, we need to put some public pressure on them. I have given a copy of my letter to the press, too."

"Well, we tried."

"Besides, Stewart, Governor Dan Mitchells is anti-union. There is talk that he made his fortune ripping-off an employee fund when he was working in the private sector. If the legislature does not stop him, he will sell off public land set aside for conservation and recreation. He says the state could benefit from the sales, and publicly owned property is Socialism. From his record, we know who would benefit from the sales."

James continued, "Fortunately, the Federal government will not let him sell federal property. Yes, Stewart, there is one other thing I want to talk to you about."

Ma Peterson gave James a look to indicate he was getting a little close to overstepping his bounds in further discussion of business on Sunday. "I am sorry Aunt Irene, this is really not business. It is something personal."

"Alright, I suppose."

"Stewart, you are looking for a job, aren't you?"

"Yes, I don't think Townsend will be asking me to come back, especially since we implicated him in the corruption charges."

"Well, I noticed you have an aptitude for legal matters. You can see the big picture. You took the initiative in your investigation, and knew what to look for. With no legal training, you seem to understand justice and legal maneuvering. You also seem to be able to discern the truth and read when people are less than forthcoming toward you. I need to hire an investigator who would also be interested in being a legal clerk with the desire of apprenticing into the law profession. The money would not pay quite as well as construction work, at first but I could maybe find some expense money to offset that until you get enough experience and pass the bar."

"When do I start?"

"How about tomorrow?"

Chapter Sixteen

LIFE AND DEATH IN DISCOVERY

Raymond started attending church with Victoria the week after he proposed to her. She also suggested that he take instruction classes so he could "join the church." Then, they would be of the same "faith." Each Sunday morning, he found himself dreading the service a little more, but he could not place his trepidations on any specific factor. As a benefit, it was a few more hours that he got to spend with her each week and less solitary time on the weekend.

Raymond ate breakfast in the dining room and stopped by to walk Victoria to church. As they walked, he asked, "Do you enjoy going to church?"

"Yes, for the most part."

"Isn't your dad going today?"

"He has some things to do at the office this morning. He is leaving for Wellspring this afternoon."

"But he doesn't go other weeks either. Why does your dad usually not attend?"

"Oh, he attends regularly on Christmas and Easter."

As they found their pews, Raymond noticed that about half of the women were there with the children or alone. Like Mr. Thomas, the other half of the men must have found something better to do on Sunday. Reverend Pharris liked to wear the long black traditional robe for service. He also chose two hymns before the message and used the same hymn each week for the "recessional" after the message. With announcements and an Old and New Testament scripture reading, he kept the entire service to within an hour. He did not want people getting bored with church.

As Reverend Pharris stood to give the message, he cleared his throat and gave a solemn look to the congregation. "There was once a man who went out in the morning to hire some workers for his vineyard. He went to the town square and retained all the men who were looking for work. He told the workers, they would work for a dollar a day. He went out about noon and did the same. He still needed more workers, so he went out again around mid-afternoon.

"The workers who were hired early in the day began discussing working conditions with workers who were hired later in the day. When those who were hired in the morning and at noon heard that the workers hired late in the day would be getting a dollar, they were getting excited. They reasoned to themselves, 'If they worked two hours for one dollar, we should be getting about four dollars, or even two dollars for the day.'

"When the workers who were hired in the morning received their pay, they grumbled, 'What, we worked the whole day for one dollar and you hired these people who only worked part of the day and received one dollar!'

"The employer answered and said, 'Is it not my money to do with as I please? Are you envious because I am generous with my money?'

"So the moral of the story is primarily - don't grumble at work. Keep your earnings to yourself. Be good and honor authority. Follow the rules of the church and society. Secondly, God has appointed your boss over you. Respect and appreciate him and his generosity. God places each of us in our station in life. May God bless you throughout the week."

They sang the closing song that they sang every week as Reverend Pharris made his way to the back of the church to greet the people as they filed out. On the way home Raymond felt empty and wondered why. He knew Victoria's cooking would cheer him up.

Mr. Thomas came home in time for lunch. Victoria asked Raymond why he was so quiet. He said, "I don't know. When I was growing up, I seemed to get more out of going to church. We sang songs that were a little livelier. The pastor taught from the Bible rather than relaying stories that were only loosely related to

Scripture or a parable that Jesus had taught. It seems the pastor always gets around to 'honoring your boss.'

At this Mr. Thomas blew up, "So you don't think you should respect your boss?"

"I didn't say that. I just think church ought to be about more spiritual substance. You don't even like to go to church."

"I am the biggest contributor to support this church. My attendance is none of your business. The pastor helps people accept and adjust to their position in life."

Victoria interjected, "Don't you two think you should take a breath and calm down?"

Raymond, who avoided confrontation at all costs, was wound up and could not control what he was saying. "Do you think we should attempt to improve our station in life? Should we not try to make the work place safer and more enjoyable for our employees?"

"You know reformers and socialists do not make good bosses!"

"I assure you, I am neither a socialist nor a reformer. I just think we should make life pleasant for others when we can."

"I have had enough of this! You and your Progressive boyfriend can talk all you want, but I advise you: Don't bite the hand that feeds you!"

"Sir, you are talking about a social gospel - one that simply keeps the people under control and is used by the government and big business."

Mr. Thomas got up and stormed out. Raymond and Victoria just sat and stared, looking stunned. "I am sorry. I didn't mean to set him off."

"Raymond, if you plan to continue working for Father, you better show some respect."

"I do respect him. Am I not allowed to have an opinion or state my beliefs?"

"Not when they conflict with Father's."

Mr. Thomas went over to the depot. Winston was there, too. He was done at the mine, since he only hired on as a "consultant" to supervise the installation and implementation of the Ingersoll, or "Widow Maker," as they called it. They were to meet Mr. Connor at the spur in Junction as he was there "advising" another mine owner.

Winston asked, "What are you so mad about?"

Mr. Thomas replied, "Oh, that future son-in-law of mine is starting to sound like a bleeding heart Progressive. Did you hear any talk in the mines, Winston? You have been there three weeks."

"No, they were still careful around me. They were not quite sure I was just a temporary consultant to get the "Widow Maker" up and running. I do have a question, though. Why do you have shoring on ten feet at the start of number five, and about twenty feet in, it starts to go to five foot sections?"

"I don't know. I always insist on ten feet. I don't want to waste man power and material cutting twice as much shoring as is necessary."

They engaged in small talk and passed the pocket flask for the two hour ride to Junction. Mr. Connor boarded and sat with them in the facing seats. "Connor, will you be able to get me those life insurance policies I requested?"

"Yes. A policy on you. One on Raymond. Both naming Victoria as the beneficiary. One on Victoria, naming you as the beneficiary.

Now you know suicide rules these out. You're not thinking suicide are you?"

"Don't be ridiculous! There was no trouble with the one-hundred-thousand dollar amount? They are all legal?"

"Yes. We can get the papers signed and the checks written this week."

Back at the house, Raymond became concerned. "Victoria, I am not sure what your dad might do. I love you and I want to marry you. Let's run off next weekend and elope."

"Raymond, that is a crazy idea! You know I want Father's blessing and a church wedding with Reverend Pharris."

"That might be, but you are the only person who can handle your dad. He might not like it at first, but I am sure he would not mind saving money rather than paying for an expensive ceremony."

As Raymond talked, Victoria surprisingly found herself thinking it might not be a bad idea. She thought her father would come around and have to forgive her at some point. She remembered what Uncle Michael used to say, "Sometimes, it is better to ask for forgiveness than permission."

Knock, knock. "I wonder who that could be."

As Victoria answered the door, there was a man outside, close to her father's age. He looked very ragged and was carrying a cane that looked more like a walking stick or a crutch. "Can I help you?"

"I sure hope so, Princess."

Victoria brightened. There was only one person who would call her princess. "Uncle Michael, is that you? I didn't recognize you until I heard your voice. Come in!"

As Michael came in, he noticed Raymond. Victoria said, "Excuse my manners. This is my fiancé, Raymond. This is my Uncle Michael."

"I am glad meet you."

"Likewise."

"Sit down, Uncle Michael. We have some catching-up to do."

"I won't be comfortable sitting down until I do what I came to do."

"What is that?"

"I have to make amends with your dad."

"That won't be possible today. He left for Wellspring and will be gone all week. He left here in a huff."

"What happened?"

"Oh, Raymond got into a disagreement with him."

"Well, you knew that was inevitable."

"Yes, but I thought Father would mellow with age. He seems to be getting more cantankerous. What brings you here?"

"Well, like I was saying, I need to make amends with your dad."

"Uncle Michael, Father said you abandoned him after stealing a load of silver. I always said you probably had a good reason. After a while, I was not even allowed to mention your name."

Victoria fixed Michael some dinner. Michael spent the afternoon telling his story about how he and Edward had their falling out. Victoria noticed how much different Michael's approach sounded compared to her father's version. Obviously, their perceptions of the fact differed, but Michael never sounded accusatory or judgmental. Father, on the other hand, had nothing good to say about Michael. She knew they could not both be right about something that was so different in their perspectives. Michael sounded more credible, since he had removed the emotion from his argument and even sounded forgiving.

Michael, in his nurturing manner, encouraged Victoria to be honest with her feelings. "Princess, your feelings are neither right nor wrong. They are just feelings. You have been suppressing your emotions so long, you need to let them out with people you can trust. Once you realize the depths of your feelings, you can decide what to do with them."

Suddenly, Victoria realized she had been denying her deepest fears. She realized she had been living under the misguided assumption that she could change her father. She even wondered if her mom died because she had lived in a state of hopeless despair. With this revelation, Victoria, who was always rational, even to a fault, broke down and sobbed.

She was overjoyed to discover Michael was still alive. She was thankful for her new found love in Raymond, and yet conscious that she did not want to lean on Raymond as a crutch or as an escape from her present reality.

Victoria finally asked, "How do you plan to make amends with Father?"

"I am here to forgive your dad, and to ask for his forgiveness."

"What do you need to be forgiven of?"

"I let my anger get the best of me. I was mad enough to kill him. That was why I fled. I figured I didn't need to be around people if I could get that mad."

Toward evening the three realized they were getting hungry. All those emotions and crying had a cathartic and draining effect. Victoria decided she would put Michael up at the inn until tomorrow. She would then get one of the worker's cabins ready for him to stay as long as he wanted. They would deal with her father when he got home. Michael warned, "Of course, he is going to say I came in and stirred all this up."

On Monday, Victoria got Michael situated. She told him she had an idea for a job he could do. The week at the mine seemed to go extremely well. Raymond noticed that without the threat of Mr. Thomas hanging over his head, he and the workers worked harder and felt lighter of spirit and livelier than usual. They also noticed that the absence of Winston made things seem to go better.

By Wednesday morning Victoria was an emotional train wreck. In the absence of her father, she realized that she was not under the usual stress that she experienced. He had been gone before, but she had always concerned herself with running the mines so she would receive his approval upon his return.

After Michael's gentle nurturing, she realized she did not want to please her father any more. In fact, she now wanted to establish her independence. She only wished she did not have a lingering doubt that she might be using Raymond to do so. After all, it was not independence if it depended upon someone else to accomplish it. She rationalized, "I do love Raymond, though."

That evening Victoria made supper for Michael and Raymond. She said she was afraid to ask Reverend Pharris to marry them as he might try to delay the ceremony until

Mr. Thomas returned. She said she had been checking and there was a justice of the peace in Junction. She could wire down and arrange a Saturday afternoon ceremony. They could stay over at the inn in Junction, have a short honeymoon and return on Sunday, ready for the work week. Raymond had no objections. Michael was reluctant to be part of a scheme that would definitely set Mr. Thomas off again. He agreed he would go down and witness the ceremony, and return Saturday evening, but with reservations. It was a plan!

Raymond thought the next two and a half days of work were the longest days he had ever experienced. Finally, Saturday came! He met Michael and Victoria at the depot. They went to Junction, met the justice of the peace and had the ceremony. Michael shook Raymond's hand, kissed the bride and headed back for Discovery on the next train.

The next day, as Victoria and Raymond boarded the train, they saw Mr. Thomas. They forgot there was only one train on Sunday. He obviously looked shocked to see them and didn't need any explanation of what had happened. He listened for a moment and got up and stormed off to the club car. After he left, Victoria said, "He will have to get over this. I am tired of him having his own way about everything."

Raymond and Victoria stayed in his room at the inn on Sunday night. The next day at work, Mr. Thomas acted as though nothing had ever happened. He coldly said, "Good morning" to Victoria as she started her work day. He called for Raymond first thing in the morning to come to the office. He said he checked the mines and found, in tunnel five, that the shoring timbers had crept down to five feet on spacing instead of ten feet. He instructed Raymond that he would be placing the timbers at ten feet or find other work. He said, "The days of mollycoddling these workers are over."

After Raymond left the office, Victoria came in and said, "You have somebody who wants to talk to you."

Before Mr. Thomas could ask who it was or what he wanted, Michael walked into the office.

"Hello, Brother."

"Just when things seemed they couldn't get worse. You come strolling in, probably wanting a handout. I should have figured you were behind my daughter's coup."

"I had nothing to do with that. I came to ask for your forgiveness and to forgive you."

"I can understand why you would want my forgiveness, but what do you have to forgive me of? "

"I forgive you for cheating and slandering me. I ask for your forgiveness for getting so mad at you that I was contemplating on how to do you in."

Victoria interjected, "Michael will be staying in town."

"Alright, I am forgiven. Now get the hell out of my office! You better stay out of my way and my family's business!"

As Raymond returned to the mines, he wondered when Mr. Thomas had time to go to the mines and check the shoring unless he went down during the middle of the night. When Raymond told the workers, they objected, but understanding the gravity of the situation, began placing the shoring timbers at ten feet.

By Friday, they had made great progress with the use of the Widow Maker. They also had a couple of extra men to clear debris who were freed from cutting and placing timbers and hand chiseling. Right after lunch the men went back into the shaft. As they started drilling, they could hear the earth settling and groaning. Some dust began to sift through the cracks in the cavern. The first man out rang the alarm and shouted, "Everybody out!"

As Raymond was shutting down the compressor, Mr. Thomas arrived on the scene. The men looked at him and started walking away. He told Raymond to get them back. Raymond just looked at him, in shock. Mr. Thomas shouted, "Alright! If you want to get back on my good side and save your job, get in there and get that Ingersoll!"

Raymond, who was usually cautious, acted upon impulse. He wanted to get back into the good graces of Mr. Thomas. As he found his way back into the cavern and reached for the Ingersoll, there was a rumbling like none of them had ever experienced.

Chapter Seventeen

RESTORATION

In Wellspring, Stewart found that he loved his new job. There were growing pains that were the greatest challenge of his life, but the rewards were also great. He actually felt as if he was headed in the right direction with his life and he was able to help people with their problems. When Stewart got to the boarding house that night, he had a letter from home. His mom and dad said they talked to Raymond's parents and he stayed in Discovery. He got a job in the mines and he found a girl. Stewart was relieved that Raymond was safe. He smiled and thought, "'He found a girl.' That is the main reason he stayed up there."

James had a meeting every morning to discuss pending cases, research and investigation results and changes in available evidence on which Stewart might be working. James said, I received a response from governor Mitchells. He read the last paragraph:

"Thank you for your recent correspondence. I have considered your request. Although their methods may appear to be severe, at times, the Pinkertons provide a valuable service. They keep business producing and maintain a level of public peace and safety that might be disrupted if labor disputes were allowed to go unregulated. Therefore, I find no grounds to appoint a special prosecutor in the above described matters."

Stewart said, "You know, if bosses and officials have to use violence and deception, maybe what they are trying to hold on to doesn't really belong to them."

"That is true. So, that is that. I still believe the public concern that is beginning to develop over the press release might have some impact on the future. In another matter, can you be able to go out of town for a few days on Wednesday? "

"Sure, what are we doing?"

"I got a notice from the justice of the peace in Junction that a young couple wants us to come up and file an injunction against her father for unsafe mining practices, and possible child labor violations. There is also a matter of replevin or recovering property that was illegally taken from another party. Since the laws are ambiguous on this matter, she relayed her concerns to the J.P. He told her he would contact a law firm in Wellspring. We will be going up and conducting a deposition."

Stewart was excited. This would be a chance to get back into the mountains and not have to walk the distance. He figured Discovery was a small town, so he had no doubt he would be seeing Raymond.

Edward Thomas received notification that a deposition would be conducted on Friday, regarding the injunction Victoria had filed when she went to Junction to get married. He abruptly left town to go to Wellspring to talk to Robert Connor and make sure he or one of his employees would be available for the deposition.

Stewart met James at the station. They boarded the train and stowed their luggage. "You don't mind if we work while we ride, do you? It'll be about a six hour trip."

As the train started moving Stewart looked out the windows to see town from the height of the train window. He enjoyed the bumping and clattering, the smell of coal and wood burning, and the rhythmic rocking of the train.

When they arrived in Discovery, they made their way to the inn dining room to eat and meet with Victoria. Stewart could not wait to find Raymond and ask who he had met. Stewart also realized that Victoria was Michaels' niece and he wanted to ask about Michael. When they finally finished, Stewart asked, "How is your Uncle Michael?"

With a surprised look, Victoria answered, "Fine, how do you know him?"

"I am Stewart. I spent the winter with him."

Victoria took Stewart and James to the one room school house which had a small attached cabin for the head master. "He lives here. He is the school master."

"I should have known. He has always been a teacher. Now he is one officially."

Michael and Stewart talked for an hour. Stewart asked, "What are you teaching the children?"

"I'm teaching them some classical literature like Dickens. We started with *Hard Times* and *Bleak House*. I'm also teaching them some American History. They love my Rough Rider accounts. We are doing some calculations, grammar and a little science. We get to teach them about an hour of Bible reading with discussion every day. I have them work through the answers themselves. I am showing them the difference between education and indoctrination."

Stewart smiled a reflective smile that seemed to exude respect and said, "I studied that curriculum all winter."

Michael continued, "Miss Victoria comes over and teaches the young ones some crafts and such for about an hour every afternoon.

I take the older students to the furniture factory and teach some woodworking. I want them to have options other than just blind acceptance of going into the mines for their futures."

Stewart asked, "Do you remember our talk about restoration?"

"You mean recovering the years the gnawing locusts have eaten, exposing the wrong, and restoring the wronged?" Michael asked.

"So, the woodcutter has been revived!"

Michael exclaimed, "Boy, I feel like I have died and gone to heaven!"

Stewart and James finally went back to their rooms to get some sleep. It had been a very long day. The next morning, at breakfast Stewart asked Victoria if she had met a man named Raymond in town. She looked down and attempted to conceal her grief. Yes, I have. I can take you to him.

After breakfast, they made their way to the opening of number five tunnel. The rocks and debris were still visible in the cavern. There was a sign that read: "Here lies Raymond. He found perfect peace."

Victoria explained that the men had attempted to clear the mine for three days. They knew after that, by the location and intensity of the slide, that he would not have survived. From the position of the slide, they knew he took the brunt of it. They changed their efforts from rescue to recovery. They knew that further efforts might place the rescuers in danger. Reluctantly they called off the search and made the cave a tomb.

She also told them how she had married Raymond. Stewart and Victoria attempted to comfort each other. She said, "This will change our case from an injunction to a wrongful death claim against Mr. Thomas."

They went back to the dining room at the inn. Stewart took meticulous notes while James talked to Victoria and prepared her for the deposition. After supper, James approached Mr. Connor and Winston, who were also staying at the inn and getting supper in the dining room. "We received information today that will make

this deposition for a wrongful death suit rather than to obtain an injunction. Do you want to proceed with the deposition, even though the suit has not been filed, or do you want us to go back to Wellspring, file and then reconvene?"

"No, let's go ahead and get it over with."

"Will you inform your client?"

"We will. He returned from Wellspring with us."

"Thank you."

The next morning, James, Stewart and Victoria came into the mining office to hold the deposition in the conference room. Robert Connor came out of Mr. Thomas's office as white as a sheet, pointing back toward Mr. Thomas's desk and the floor. There, on the floor was Edward Thomas. He was already ashen gray, with a trickle of blood formed under each nostril.

James and Stewart ran in to see if they could help. James said, "He is alive. We need to get him to a bed as close by as possible. Do you have a doctor in town?"

Victoria said, "Let's take him home."

The men recruited a couple of miners who were passing by the office on the sidewalk. They sent another man for the doctor. They carried Edward to his home and placed him in the bed in the guest room on the lower level rather than attempting to carry him up the stairway.

Edward Thomas was paralyzed. He could only blink his eyes. Victoria asked him questions. "Father, if you can understand me, blink twice."

He blinked twice. It appeared he could understand her. Michael had been informed of the situation and came into the room.

"Father, I have held you responsible for Raymond's death. I am trying to forgive you, but I don't know if I will be able to do so."

She could see a tear well up in Edward's eyes and overflow down his cheek. Michael stood beside her and held her hand. "I have decided I will not pursue the wrongful death law suit, but there is a trade-off. I am going to have Mr. Peterson and Mr. Taylor draw up an agreement that you will start giving dividends to the miners who have been your loyal employees all these years. You and I will retain fifty percent – your split at thirty percent and mine at twenty percent. The miners will receive percentages depending upon the number of years they have worked for us."

The tears had stopped flowing from Mr. Thomas's eyes. They now stood open with a look of horror. Victoria continued, "There is one other matter. Uncle Michael will be restored to twenty percent ownership. I know your original agreement was for him to have forty percent to your sixty percent, but your sixty percent has been reduced."

Michael objected, "Princess that is not necessary. I don't need the money or the headaches. I will be fine teaching."

"I'm sorry Uncle Michael, I have made up my mind," Victoria said as she looked at Michael through the tops of her eyes with a down-turned facial expression.

"I know that look. We will consider your proposal. Now I have something to say. Edward, you are my brother. I meant it with all my heart when I told you I forgave you. I also was sincere when I asked for your forgiveness.

"The stories about me and ignoring me were the easy parts. The fact that you could just turn your back on your brother, that took longer. I had things I wanted to say to you, but you wouldn't even reason with me. That is truly water under the bridge. I would like to know that I am forgiven for wanting to kill you back then."

Edward closed his eyes for a brief spell and finally blinked them twice. For the next day, Victoria and Michael stayed beside Edward, reminiscing about his and Michaels' childhoods and fond memories of their parents. Victoria talked about tender remembrances of her mother and the good times the family shared. Victoria sang hymns and read Bible verses. During the night on the second day, Edward slipped away.

After Victoria regained composure, she said, "Uncle Michael, I couldn't have made it through these past few weeks without you."

"Don't' worry, Princess. I'm not going anywhere. I am right where I belong."

AFTERWORD

One of my granddaughters asked if I was going to dedicate the Woodcutter's Revival. I told her, "Of course. I am going to dedicate it to my granddaughters. She giggled with approval. I wanted to leave something of myself for my children and granddaughters.

Sure, we have made things together in the shop and at the kitchen table, but I wanted them to have some insight into my thinking. I wanted to freeze a frame in time, both the time I lived and produced and the time frame in which the story took place.

My granddaughters, in order by age, are Hannah, Hailey and Meliah. Of course, the dedication extends to their parents, my children – my daughter, Shannon, and my son, Micah. Tim and Melinda might not be my "actual" children, but they are by choice. They are also special to Shannon and Micah, not to mention the girls.

Everybody has heard people talk about the 'good old days.' I have also heard people say, Those who talk about the good old days just have a poor memory."

It is human nature to wonder if people faced less stress, enjoyed life more, or found simpler entertainment in earlier times. People also wonder how these things will be different in the future. I have personally wondered if there truly are 'good old days' or if people tend to gravitate toward romantic notions of the past because they want to believe that people had it better at some point in time.

The purpose of this book was to attempt to portray a short period in history as accurately as possible. The time chosen was toward the end of period that was the awakening of the Industrial Revolution. Imagine life one hundred years ago.

Let the reader compare and contrast the beginnings of the Industrial Revolution, with the use of steam to the progress and the resulting life styles created by the Information Age, the Internet and the computer.

Was there less stress a hundred years ago? Would the character of Michael, betrayed by his power hungry and greedy brother, Edward, have felt less pain and bewilderment a hundred years ago? When Michael charged up San Juan Hill with Teddy Roosevelt, did he have a guarantee he would survive? Were the bullets any less real than today?

The Woodcutter's Revival was an attempt to cause people to think about being born in a certain era rather than another. It was to portray betrayal and forgiveness. The story was about human ambition and greed. It compared and contrasted political leanings and leadership styles. There was even a love story found in the pages. It was an attempt at a slice of life that, hopefully did more than entertain.

ABOUT THE AUTHOR

Jerry is a retired school teacher. He graduated from Ball State University with a Master of Arts degree in Education. Jerry has been very active in various political and educational groups. He has established, administered and taught in an alternative school in Knox, known as the ACE Program. ACE stood for Alternative and Continuing Education.

Jerry has taught in Marion, Kokomo, Wanath-LaCrosse, and Knox Indiana. He has also completed administrative training and principal certification. His major focus has been education, both in the formal school setting and the life lessons we learn from living every day.

Jerry has advocated for fair treatment and voluntary self-growth and improvement for teachers. He has also owned and operated small businesses and worked for others in supervisory positions in retail sales and government military production.

Jerry is a husband, father and grandfather. He loves to travel, write and work in the wood, metal and leather shops at home. He has built and uses a wood fired pizza oven.

Jerry Slauter

ABOUT THE
ILLUSTRATOR

Scott "Doc" Wiley has been illustrating since the age of three. He has always loved to hike in the Shenandoah Mountains and take photos of the splendor of nature.

Retired from the Army, Scott served as a tank commander and combat correspondent in Viet Nam. Scott also earned a Doctorate in Art Education from Ball State University. Scott illustrated portraits of Washington and Lincoln that hang in Tippecanoe County Courthouse in Lafayette, Indiana.

More recently, Scott has served three deployments to Afghanistan. He illustrated a portrait of Patton that hangs in the Army Chief Chaplain's Office in the Pentagon. It survived the attack of 9/11. "Scott...has a passion for American History and produces detailed realistic 'etched graphite' illustrations from historical photographs. Research precedes execution."

His current projects include History of Defense Warning/ "As You Were – Life in the Field of the 11th ACRVVC." He has recently completed illustrating *The Woodcutter's Revival* for long-time friend and author, Jerry Slauter. Scott spent over 360 hours of research, planning and drawing. He also spent several hours writing narratives for each illustration. The efforts are obvious as they are on display at http://wileystudio.smugmug.com

Scott "Doc" Wiley

PROMOTE WOODCUTTER'S REVIVAL

If the Woodcutter's Revival touched you or if you believe it might be of benefit to others please share it.

You might already have ideas how to promote concepts on the Internet, such as FaceBook or Twitter. If you are enthusiastic about it, share your enthusiasm.

- Give the book as a gift.

- Write a book review for your local newspaper, magazines or web sites. Amazon reviews are particularly effective.

- Talk about the book in small groups at church, work or other social, professional or service groups.

- Give the book to church, educational, political or service organizational leaders.

- Offer several copies to women's shelter, prisons, rehabilitations homes, libraries, or any place people might enjoy a message of hope and healing.

- Post blogs in which you share part of the book that touched you the most, without giving away too much of the story. Leave a little of the intrigue so the reader can find their own experience with the woodcutter's Revival.

- If you own a business, store or shop, place a display of the books on the counter or display table to resell to customers. Books can be purchased in discounted, wholesale volumes.

- Send emails to your entire list with links to:

www.WoodCuttersRevival.com
http://wileystudio.smugmug.com

If you would like to contact the author to schedule a visit to your church or organization, go to:

www.WoodcuttersRevival.com

or email:

jerrysworldsavings@me.com